CATAPULT

STORIES EMILY FRIDLUND

SARABANDE BOOKS
LOUISVILLE. KY | BROOKLYN. NY

Copyright © 2017 Emily Fridlund

Library of Congress Cataloging-in-Publication Data

Names: Fridlund, Emily, author.
Title: Catapult : stories / by Emily Fridlund.
Description: First edition. | Louisville, KY : Sarabande Books, [2017]
Identifiers: LCCN 2017002604 (print) | LCCN 2017007179 (ebook) | ISBN
9781946448057 (pbk. : alk. paper) | ISBN 9781946448064 (ebook)
Classification: LCC PS3606.R536 A6 2017 (print) | LCC PS3606.R536 (ebook) |
DDC 813/.6--dc23
LC record available at https://lccn.loc.gov/2017002604

Interior and exterior design by Kristen Radtke.

Manufactured in Canada.
This book is printed on acid-free paper.
Sarabande Books is a nonprofit literary organization.

  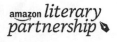

This project is supported in part by an award from the National Endowment for the Arts. The Kentucky Arts
Council, the state arts agency, supports Sarabande Books with state tax dollars and federal funding from the
National Endowment for the Art

·for my family,
who gave me love and art

Beauty is merciless and intemperate.
Who, turning this way and that, by day, by night,
still stands in the heart-felt storm of its benefit,
will plead in vain for mercy, or cry, "Put out
the lovely eyes of the world, whose rise and set
move us to death!" And never will temper it,
but against that rage slowly may learn to pit
love and art, which are compassionate.

—Mona Van Duyn,
"Three Valentines to the Wide World"

CONTENTS

Introduction by Ben Marcus

Acknowledgments
About the Author

INTRODUCTION

I wasn't too many sentences deep into Emily Fridlund's remarkable collection of short stories before I started to feel the strong pull of her intelligence. "It is easy to be wrong about a person you are used to," says the narrator of "Expecting," an eccentric portrait of familial survival. Such an admission might serve as a kind of motto for Fridlund's work. She writes of families, marriage, and childhood as if our received wisdom—what we thought we knew about life and love and family—needs reparation. Fridlund charts, with a compressed, hurtling narrative style, the inner mythologies of her people, the logic and evasions and fears that guide and overwhelm them. This is fiction as excavation, peeling away the machinery of people and converting it to narrative. Fridlund shines a spotlight on what gets hidden and unreported, and the result can be overwhelming—cutting and funny and filled with difficult truth. Hardly a line goes by in these stories without some piercing bit of wisdom or destabilizing insight, and Fridlund does this with a light, swift hand, building stories of wit and misunderstanding and loss that are spilling over with seductive revelations.

A character from "Marco Polo," speaking of his wife, says, "Once, on the Fourth of July, when our neighbors were setting off fireworks on the sidewalk outside our window, she looked at me and said, 'You look like someone I've never met.'" Love is often misfiring in such a way in these stories. Fridlund is expert at tracking what happens when two people cannot calibrate their desire, when husband and wife, boyfriend and girlfriend, friend and friend, find each other strange, difficult, remote, impossible. Characters are isolated, bereft, looking out at a world that is increasingly beyond their control. The result, grim as it sounds, emerges as a kind of comedy. It is sadly funny to read of people whose insights remove them from safety, who are stuck inside cycles of thought that bear down on them and leave them exhausted. It is the very stuff of complex, necessary fiction.

When I finished the book I felt impressed with Fridlund's range, but also her command of narrative tools, her control of the emotional atmosphere in a story. What a comfort, to read a writer so irrepressibly smart, so keen to achieve lines of prose that stun with their precision and insight. Her stories are free of inessential details, the kind of padding one too often finds in stories that bide their time until they no longer matter. This writer will make everything count, including the kind of data that is usually left for dead in a story. What is literary authority, after all, but the ability to regularly, without apparent effort, make the most of every sentence, to build feeling in every line and do it in such a way that is tough, tight, funny, and often brilliantly disruptive?

—Ben Marcus

EXPECTING

I.

My wife could take your skin off with one glance, she was that excruciating. She could call you to her with one finger. She could do long division in her head. Another thing she could do really well was sob, and I envied her this, assuming it left nothing to eat at her inside. It is easy to be wrong about a person you are used to. The day she left, she gave me an American flag packed in a clear plastic bag she broke with her teeth. I said, "What, you're going to war?" And she said, "You always wanted something to hang from the porch." She could be sweet and scornful at the same time.

A son is the same as a wife, save this confusion. These are the things my son will do: the laundry, the lawn, the bills. He has a head for numbers, like his mom, and figures our finances on spreadsheets. Kyle is nineteen, and it seems like the age he's been all his life. I can hardly remember him being anything but lanky and bearded and morose. Periodically, his girlfriend Meg lives with us. She fills the freezer with cans of Diet Dr. Pepper that bulge threateningly—aluminum balloons—and burst. At night, I scrape tiny brown ice flakes from our frozen dinners. I heat the oven to 350 and arrange cardboard dishes on a metal cookie sheet.

"No au gratin potatoes, Darrell."

I don't know when it started, but my son calls me by name. He says, Darrell, there's a call for you; Darrell, wipe your face. He says my name like it's a kelly green suit, like it's my botched attempt to be like other humans.

Because Kyle calls me Darrell, I call him Son. "Son, the potatoes come with the meal. You get what comes."

"The smell of them makes me sick. Why don't you eat them for me before I sit down? Come on, Darrell."

He is standing in the doorway, his shoulders covered in a brightly woven throw. He is bare-chested, and I can see a few orange hairs flicker about his nipples. He has a five-pound dumbbell in one hand he's been lugging around for weeks.

I take out the steaming dinners and spoon his potatoes into my rice. My son makes me unreasonably soft, like there's a rotten spot in me only he knows about. I coax him to the table by setting out an open beer. When he sits down, he balances the dumbbell up on one end next to his elbow.

"Can you get my work socks in tonight?" I talk into my food.

"They can go with the towels, I guess." He eats his chicken with a spoon.

We stay until the cardboard dishes start to collapse, then stand without speaking and throw our meals in the trash. We eat bowls of cereal. Kyle shakes a box of powdered Jell-O into his wide-open mouth.

For a few weeks after his mother left, I drove around the city on Kyle's behalf, trying to find him a job. That was early summer, just after graduation, when the days were as long as they were ever going to get. I was afraid it looked bad to have an adult son without any plans. I brought home applications from Best Buy and Walgreen's, each folded in half and tucked neatly in my lunch cooler. With my best handwriting and a new felt pen, I filled out my son's personal information: Kyle Craige-Gryzbowski, no previous retail experience. I passed these papers to him shyly, barely looking in his eyes, my fingers damp from gripping the pen. Nothing came of this, which was a worry at first, then a relief. My wife used to call him Lazy Ass, but there is something comforting about Kyle's laziness, the way a lolling cat can soothe your nerves. It pleases me to find him on the floor at the end of the day. He does halfhearted sit-ups and folds sheets. Sometimes, he's just asleep, the TV shuffling its faces around, the night coming down, so slow and quiet I'd be a fool to complain. You don't get many chances to be happy.

Of course, he can be difficult—not frightening like his mother, but frightened, which is worse. Try to see this: a six-foot man with a curly red beard who won't come out of the basement. Kyle has respect for storms. On green summer nights, he holds a radio to his head and paces the sweating cement in his socks. I tell him, "Son, there's no sirens. Come on upstairs." But Kyle has a machine that calculates dew point and wind speed. He looks me in the face and says, "Fuck you, Darrell."

On a night like this, I meet Meg at the back door. She is timid and avoids me by rubbing her eyes and yawning deeply: "God, I'm tired." Her timidity also makes her polite, so she sits down when I tell her to. "Pears?" I hold out a squat, yellow can with a foolishly beaming man on the label. "Or fruit cocktail with cherries?" I shake the other can in the air.

"Maybe a little of both?" Meg runs the roller coaster at Mall USA, so she's deft with people she dislikes. She is twenty and hasn't seen her parents since she left Culver in the eleventh grade to get a job in the Cities. She treats everyone older than her like an employer.

Truth is, I usually regret making her eat with me. She slides her pears across her plate, leaving shiny, transparent trails. She picks the fibers from her oranges. When I ask her about her day, innocently enough, she tells me about a man who vomited out of his bumper car. "Hmm," I say, clearing the plates. "Interesting." I avert my eyes from her slippery fruit.

She says, "Sometimes I get sick too."

"You coming down with something?"

"Well. I'm pregnant."

It seems important to keep clearing our plates, to do this as long as possible. I take one fork at a time. I tend to the day-old crumbs on the table.

"Mr. Gitowski?" She says my name in a rush, like she's trying to get past it to something else.

"Gryzbowski," I say, but I hold off from spelling it out. Briefly, I think about my son downstairs, listening with all his machines to changes in the atmosphere. It would seem good and correct if the wind picked up, if the digits showing barometric pressure started falling. I believe that significant events should make some impact.

"G-R-Y-Z-B-O-W-S-K-I."

"Isn't that what I said?"

I am generous with her. "Maybe. I think so."

She pushes out her chair, smiling with just her mouth. I suppose her line of work requires an official face. "Thanks for the fruit."

After my wife left, I hung her American flag from a pole on the porch and tried to summon up some patriotic feelings. During Vietnam, I was always hoping my number would come up. I was working at a factory that produced party balloons, doing quality control in a great shuddering room that felt like a force of nature. They made me wear earmuffs and gloves. I looked for balloons without puckers, balloons without holes, until I was so bored and sad that war compared favorably. Back then, I was insulted by the kind of man who wore pieces of the American flag sewed on the cuffs of his jeans. I was Kyle's age, nineteen, and I felt that killing someone would be less ghastly than selling sticky rubbers to kids. It wasn't just about balloons. It was more that I wanted to die and war seemed the kind of place you could think that without being embarrassed.

The flag is wrapped around its pole like it decided to curl up for the night. I try to unwind it, but it's caught, so I unfasten the pole from the house and take the whole thing inside. My wife would have scolded me for this. She had rules about indoor things and out; a flagpole in the living room would have made her distressed. She would have given me an exasperated look, a you-are-still-such-a-child-I-can't-even-yell-at-you look before taking the flag and marching it back outside. This was the best and worst thing about my wife: she felt sorry for me. When I put my work boots on the mantel or fell asleep on her side of the bed, she'd groan and clench her teeth. She'd kiss me, long and deep, a sigh of disappointment.

She tried out her anger on our son. I remember when Kyle was small, she'd yell at him because he wouldn't ride his bike in the summer. "Don't you want to go out with the other boys?" She asked it over and over until it turned into an accusation. When he was a teenager, she put braces on his teeth, then threw her keys at him when he was too afraid to go to the orthodontist to get them off. I said to her, "All in his own time," and she said, "Of course *you* don't mind if your son's a teenager the rest of his life." She'd glance past Kyle and me into the reaches of the house, as if looking for someone more reasonable. She had a way of touching her lips with her fingers, pinching up a bit of skin and letting go.

In the living room, I unwind the flag from its pole, smoothing it on the floor. Spread out like that, it looks like something I should lay myself across—a bedspread, a beach towel. It looks like somewhere I should sleep. Meg comes home late from work. I hear her fumble through the kitchen, and I start to stand up, but she's standing over me before I can go anywhere.

"Mr. Gryzbowski." Her ponytail is cockeyed, and it makes her head look off, swollen out slightly over her ear.

"Oh. So, there you are." I'm on my knees, gathering up the flag between my arms. "Good day at Mall USA?"

For a second I want to hide—this flag my wife gave me, my big body, my sullen American pride. I try folding the flag, but the cloth is slippery and uncooperative.

"People are stupid, you know?" Meg tugs out her hair tie, but her hair is greasy and stays where it was. "This guy? He tried to climb out of his seat in the middle of the ride. A grown man, and he's up there with all these little kids hollering at the top of his lungs."

"He was scared, right?" I drop the flag in a heap on the couch.

"Everybody's scared. It's a scary ride." She runs a hand through her hair, then sniffs her fingers. "What makes him think he's different?"

Soon Meg starts wearing shirts like hockey jerseys and eating all the best things in the house: frozen pizzas, Oreos. She watches football with me on Sunday afternoons and knows when to say "bump-and-run." I like her better now than I did. She burps when she drinks from her soda can, popping up her eyebrows every time. She reminds me of my grandfather. She sighs like he did and rests her small white hand against the fly of her jeans. I suspect there is something different about her body, but I can't say what. For a long time, it's nothing you can see, just this look on her face like she's swallowed something without chewing it first. Like she's waiting to see if she'll choke. Then one day she's big as a boat, and it startles me to walk in the living room and find her moored on the couch. I have to keep myself from staring. I have to fasten my gaze on a clump of brown hair she holds between her teeth.

Meg spits out the hair and says nothing. She looks devastated by her body. I tell her she looks nice because I'm afraid for her.

"Oh. Well." She doesn't give me her official face. She smiles in a way that makes me think she hasn't considered it first.

Then Kyle comes in—barefoot, wearing black biking gloves— and she turns official again. It's not her Mall USA self, but a girlishness she assumes just for my son. She rolls her eyes at him when he wedges his way in between the armrest and her body. She nudges him with her elbow, managing to look—as teenage girls so often do—simultaneously superior and deprived.

Kyle rolls a hefty dumbbell onto her lap. "Lift it."

"Whatever."

Kyle is grave. "I've moved up to ten pounds. Darrell, you try."

I watch Kyle drag the dumbbell off Meg's lap. She says he's hurting her. He calls her a wimp. When he gets the thing in his hand, he purses his lips and squints his eyes in exaggerated exertion. They're always acting like this, like they've been forced to sit next to each other in class and they don't know whether they should fight or show off.

I say, "Let's see *you*, Son," but he sets the dumbbell on the floor and shakes out his wrist.

"Naw. I've done my reps already." He pushes up his sleeve and flexes his bicep. "You can touch it, it's real hard."

I don't know if he's talking to Meg or me. We both reach out and poke at his arm, prodding the little lump awakened there. For a second I feel thrown off, as if Kyle is the pregnant one, and we're feeling him for signs of new life. Then his fist trembles and he brushes us away.

"Oh, what a strong man!" Meg grabs at his hand as he tries to tuck it under his armpit. They wrestle for a moment on the couch, Meg reaching around the dome of her belly. Kyle is giddy and confident. It seems he's worked all this out: Meg's pregnancy, her need for him, her colossal body. He tries to shirk her off, and still she snatches at his arm, holding on till he cringes with pleasure.

For a few weeks at the end of the summer Meg stays with us every night. She takes half-hour showers after work and makes Dr. Pepper popsicles in the ice tray, milky brown cubes she sucks between her fingers. When she gets too big to share Kyle's single bed, I offer her the one in the master bedroom. I stay in Kyle's room, in a sleeping bag on his box spring, and Kyle gets the mattress on the floor. I'm in charge of dinner—I try casseroles now, Hamburger Helper—and Meg does the dishes because she says we leave spots. Kyle makes the shopping list. None of us takes out the trash. It molders under the sink, a dense, vegetable stink, until I eventually drag it out into the backyard. When I lose the toothpaste cap, Meg scolds me and Kyle backs her up, so I can't tell anymore which parts we're supposed to play: who's the parent here, who's the wife, who's the child. In the evenings, we gather in the living room where we watch *Nova* and fall asleep. First Kyle, then Meg, then me, the universe on TV bending into flexible strings and vibrating softly.

II.

The thing about the baby is she isn't a baby at all. We all see this right away. She is serious and disapproving, watching us blunder about her with bottles of formula, with nests of wet diapers. We take to hiding things from her. When we misplace her pacifier, we give her a toothbrush instead. We try to convince her that this is what babies do, suck on the bristly ends of little sticks, but the baby won't bite. It's not that we don't like the baby, it's that she doesn't like us.

"Agg," she says a lot, her face a grim frown of disappointment. She turns to us when we speak, listening with all her might for something she can endorse. She looks like a disgruntled old man, her ears red, her scalp bald and splotchy. Whenever I'm alone with her, she assesses my parenting with an intractable glare.

We're out of clean spoons, and I offer her mashed peas from a fork, but she closes her lips primly.

"Come on," I say. "It's how everybody eats."

She knows better. She knows that five-month-old babies have toothless mouths that are unsuited for metal tines. I find a wooden baking spoon, and she licks green mush from its tip grudgingly.

She'd make us feel better if she'd cry. When Kyle was a baby he used to scream in his crib all night, banging his elbows against the wooden bars and denying us sleep. We resented him in the usual ways, his mother and I, rolling our eyes and humoring him with songs about crowded barnyards. This baby humors *us*. Once, I found Meg bent over the crib, the baby's onesie in a twist around her head, the baby's naked body doing an underwater swim through Meg's hair. Meg was crying and the baby was not. "I'm doing my best," Meg defended herself, and the baby said, "Hmmm."

I suspect that the baby has things to say she's holding back. She parcels out a syllable at a time, polite baby talk, but her expressions are complex sentences.

For instance, she wrinkles up her nose at me, saying: Come now, wash your hands; use warm water and pat your fingers dry so when you touch my soft baby skin you don't alarm me.

She clenches her jaw in the parking lot, saying: No sirree. If you leave me in my stroller while you pay the parking meter, who knows where I'll be when you get back. I may consort with criminals. I may offer myself to kidnappers and feral dogs.

She is hardest on Kyle, though he doesn't know it yet. When he holds her, he's fond of moving her limbs up and down like levers. He cranks her arms, bending her elbows open and closed as if testing to see if she works properly. She looks at him like he's an idiot, like he's a very crazy man who must be indulged with the greatest of patience. When she can't take any more, she puffs out her baby cheeks and drools on his sleeve.

"Agg," Kyle says, using the baby's language. He's proud of her words and is always looking for contexts in which he can use them. "Blah."

Kyle's look of distaste is in fact a look of pleasure: the baby's is real. She reminds me of my wife with this look, and I pray that the baby will never learn to talk, never wobble onto her feet so she can walk away. She disapproves of us, but for the time being there is nothing she can do. We take pictures of her, posed helplessly in our arms, while we can.

We call her "the baby" to her face to make ourselves feel better. *Does the baby want upsie upsie? Is the baby a sleepyhead?*

Once, we take her to the park so she can see everything she can't
do: climb the jungle gym like the neighborhood boys, wade barefoot
into the lake with the little girls. We take her rowing in a rental boat,
and I make a show of pulling at the oars. "Look at this," I say, rowing fast and hard, propelling that boat across the pond until I'm wet
with sweat and panting heavily. "Look at this," Kyle says, standing
up and waving his arms. He rocks the boat under his feet so we bob
and toss through the green skim of milfoil. The baby, quiet on Meg's
lap, is unimpressed. For a few minutes she watches us in her bored
and haughty way, and then she's distracted by a goose hissing nearby.
Look, look! I want to say, rowing the boat in circles around the lily
pads, sinking the oars into the slick fronds so they come up laden.
I want to say, *You're nothing at all, you're eighteen pounds in someone's
arms, you're a dead weight that would sink to the bottom of the pond and
drift over carp and rotting cattails.* I want to say, *We're all you got,* but
Meg talks first, saying, "I'm hot. I'm fucking dying."

Kyle and I stare at her. We despise her for not even trying to
look good in front of the baby.

Kyle says, "We still got twenty minutes with the boat."

I say, "We're just getting started."

Meg rearranges the baby on her lap, hefting her up and putting
her back like she's considering her options. "Listen!" She sounds
whiny. "I'm *hot*. I need to get the hell *out*."

Kyle blinks at her. "Get out then."

Meg turns on him. "We're in a lake, what do you want me to do?
I've got the goddamn baby."

She seems surprised to find herself yelling, and the baby does
too. They glance apprehensively at each other, like old rivals who've
been pretending to get along for the sake of decorum. They both
have their hands in fists.

When we get to shore, Meg deposits the baby in my arms so she
can go buy herself an iced latte. She holds the waxed cup in one
hand and a plastic straw in the other, spinning fast circles in the
ice. Periodically, she tilts the cup into her mouth, the ice sticking,

then sliding in a swift blow against her teeth. She lags behind on the walk back, chewing the ice and rim of the cup and the tip of the plastic straw. By the time we're home, the cup is in shreds and she won't go in the front door. She sits for a long time on the hood of her car, jiggling her heels against the bumper.

She bends the straw into an accordion and fits it in her mouth. I know she will leave soon and not come back.

Once when Kyle was a boy, my wife bought him a puppy, a Rottweiler mix with crooked ears. At first it was just a drooling, piddling, wiggling lump, but its development was so fierce that within a week it knew to sit for its food and wet the papers by the door. Within a month it was rolling over on demand, and it seemed that its education could go on and on, that it could learn anything we chose to teach it. It seemed the puppy became a dog so fast that it might become something else after that: a circus performer, a kindergarten student.

A human is different. A human lies there in your arms, month after month, feeble, sucking her own fingers. A human baby stays a squirming lump of flesh—uncoordinated, uncooperative—and needs you to lug her around and fill her with food and scrape excrement from her thighs. A baby stays this way so long, it seems improbable that she will be something else anytime soon, impossible that she will grow long and thin, her bones knobbing out from under her skin, her legs capable of carrying her. It seems unlikely that she will ever be anything but passive, inert, yours.

III.

Kyle tucks the baby under his arm and carries her around the house. He sets her up on the table when he's writing out the bills, giving her a ballpoint pen which she bangs against her knee. He props her against the bathroom mirror when he brushes his teeth. He doesn't lug around his dumbbell anymore, not since Meg left for design school in Duluth, not since the baby works just as well for building up his muscles. He balances her little bottom on his palm and raises her high above his head. When she wobbles up there, he makes a grab at her with his other hand and brings her gracefully into his chest.

In the kitchen, Kyle slides the baby around in a laundry basket—over the crinkly linoleum and under the table, where she drapes herself in his undershirts while he finishes his lunch. He stuffs his whole sandwich in his mouth, bulging out his eyes, peering down at her in her blue plastic cage. He puffs out his cheeks and sprinkles a few crumbs on her face, trying to impress her.

"Agg," he murmurs through his food, doting, adoring. "Agg agg, hmmm."

"Wow," the baby says.

"What?"

"Wow."

The baby has never used an English word before, and Kyle regards her with alarm. He looks at her like she's cursed him, like she's making fun of him, like she's a defiant puppy that's learned to talk.

He swallows hard, wiping his face. "Honey, it's me. I'm the baby's Daddy."

And the baby says, all sarcasm and scorn: "Wow."

"Darrell?" He looks up at me, sitting with my Velveeta sandwich across the table.

I do my best to reassure him. "It's just another sound she makes. She has no idea what she's saying."

It only happens once. We lose the baby somewhere in the house. She crawls off when we're watching *Nova* and we spend twenty minutes looking in closets and under beds. She's just a baby: she has stout, flabby arms and legs she drags around like an amphibian sea creature. There are no pads on her feet—just soft, pink flesh—and still she manages to get away.

Kyle loses his head, rifling through the laundry basket and tossing boxer shorts across the room. He puts his face in the baby's

Winnie-the-Pooh pajamas like he's a dog taking in her scent. He wraps the pajamas around his neck and stalks down the hall and back, too upset to look for her effectively.

I search as methodically as I can. I pluck back the curtains and check behind the couch, pressing my palms into the carpet so they come up mottled. I sink my arms into the closet coats, into the wool and fleece, all those wintery fabrics closing in on me. Hangers catch against my throat. My wife could find anything lost, can opener in a baking dish, keys in a flowerpot. She'd know exactly where a baby would be, and she'd go there as well, to that secret place where no one else could find her. For a second, I think about how my wife looked the night she left for Tucson. I think about her sitting on the bed in her new green swimsuit, breasts sagging into points in the pockets of her bikini. She had goose pimples. When she smiled sadly, her lips whitened. A hanger clatters to the ground, and I fight past hoods and sleeves to the very back of the closet. I touch children's snowsuits, clingy cocktail dresses.

I push out of the dark and try to be practical. I ask Kyle, "Did you check in the kitchen? In that weird corner of the cabinet?"

"You think she's in a soup pot?"

"How about behind the radiator where the dog hid his balls?"

"Fuck you, Darrell." Kyle presses the pajamas to his face. He strides up and down the hallway in his helpless way, as if the baby's disappearance is a storm to wait out. I go into the bathroom to escape his dread.

And there she is. In the bathtub, standing behind the half-drawn curtain with its gray mildew blossoms. She has one hand on each metal faucet, tugging thoughtfully, humming to herself. She's pulled off her diaper, and her bare ass is the same creamy white as the porcelain.

"Oh!" For an instant, she embarrasses me. I have an impulse to close up the shower curtains and let her go about her business. I have an impulse to back away and let her undress, let her draw her bath, soak her bald body in warm water, wash the dirt from her fingernails, shampoo the downy hair on her head, dress, call a cab, and get away. I say, "I'm sorry," and she looks up, startled, distraught. She looks at me like my apology is not enough, my presence a disappointment beyond words.

Then Kyle swoops in and lifts her up under the armpits, so her face breaks. "C'mon!" she says, and I can see her considering her options: she thinks about kicking her legs, biting his cheek, pounding his arms. She decides to reason with him instead. "C'mon," she suggests, pleading at first, then indignant. "C'mon, c'mon, c'mon."

Kyle folds her into his arms, and though she struggles to sit up, to raise her head, he holds her on her back like she's a newborn. "C'*mon!*" she says, but Kyle's trembling all over and he will never listen to her.

IV.

Meg comes by on one of the last cold days of a very cold spring. The flag flicks in the wind, and my wife's hyacinths bulge out of the ground like bumpy green grenades. Meg, in my doorway, has her fists in her jacket pockets, her hood blown up and flattened against her cheek. She looks for all the world like a little girl who's come to ask my son to play.

"Mr. Gitowski?" she says, and I find myself nervous to see her. I hang my body in the doorframe, two palms against the cool wood, looking down at her as best I can.

"I—" She smiles in a flash. "I just wanted to see how everything's going."

"Right."

"She's getting really big?"

"The baby?"

"Yeah."

I feel defensive. "She's still little. You know."

"Talking a lot?"

I sigh, closing my arms over my chest. "Some."

Meg peers past me into the dark of the house. She unpeels the hood from her head, and I see a smattering of acne on her chin, red and glazed in a shiny make-up. "Can I see her?"

I hold my breath for a half second. "Well. Of course."

Inside I tell Meg to wait by the umbrella hook. It's where my wife used to have the UPS man stand, or the pizza boy when he came with a warm cardboard box balanced on a palm. Meg backs into the radiator and touches a zit on her chin with the tip of her pinkie finger.

I slip into the baby's room and peer into her crib. She's sleeping with her knees curled up against her chest, several strands of orange hair plastered to her forehead. She opens her eyes when I touch her, blinking blearily. She sits up, raises a hand to her head, and carefully brushes the hair from her face. She tugs her shirt over her exposed belly. When I pick her up, her legs swing down over my hips and bump the backs of my thighs.

Back in the entryway, I pass her over to Meg. "The baby. Here."

"Oh!" Meg looks frightened by her. The baby hangs from her arms.

The baby says, "Agg."

"Look at you!" Meg breathes. "You're all grown up!"

And the baby—weary, worn out—says, "Come *on*."

CATAPULT

That summer I was reading vampire books, so when Noah said no to sex, I let myself pretend that's what he was. I told myself: inside his mouth is a hallway to death. That's why his teeth are so wet, so flashy. Sometimes when he talked, I could see a white Cert floating over his tongue, flicking in and out of sight like the smallest of buoys. I wanted him to save me. I wanted him to save me from myself. It occurred to me for the first time that summer that I might have had a difficult life before I met him. There was a rusted yellow truck in front of my house; inside, painfully yellow linoleum. His house across the highway was neat as a table setting. He had a magical symmetrical family: mother, father, sister, terrier. He had a baby grand piano, a square of wallpaper in a frame, and a living room whose whole fourth wall was a mirror. Facing the back of the house, you could see the front door with its diamond glass, and through it, the well-intentioned geometry of streets upon streets.

Instead of having sex, we built a catapult in the grass. What else could we do? We were fourteen. Childhood was almost all we'd ever known. Every awkward pause brought us back to it. With relief, defeat, we sat on the driveway with the last Lego man in a

Dixie cup. His face was just three dots—eye, eye, and mouth—and I remember thinking, What more, *what more* does anyone need? We launched three-dot man over the grass with wonderfully perfected, systematic, almost rote ambition. Over and over again. Childhood, by then, had been sucked dry by the unremitting soullessness of adolescence.

We'd met in class. In April, Noah had taken out a pencil and set it on the floor beneath my desk. It lay like a hieroglyph for me to decipher or ignore. It was too deliberate to be addressed, and I felt stunned by my advantage. I'd practiced for this moment of superiority all my life. In a hundred mirrors, I had looked out from under my shelf of bangs and said: You could never understand me. But when the bell rang, he stood up as if no such thing as a pencil had ever existed—as if pencils were the stuff of nerdy fantasy novels, of speculative documentaries—and, bewildered, humiliated, I touched his sleeve. "Is that yours?"

This made him tuck in his pants, which were already tucked. I could see the misshapen wad of fabric beneath his belt that was the bottom part of his shirt. "No."

"Yes," I told him. My bangs were a roof, and I sat under them, waiting. I wanted him to admit that he was the one who laid the trap.

He held on tight to his backpack straps.

"You put it there," I said. "*You* dropped it."

"Want some lunch?" He took the pencil back. Like a good vampire living among humans, he acted as if he'd seen all this human work turn to wreckage before. He was patiently waiting it out, letting it crumble of its own accord.

At lunch I noticed his beautiful hands. Every time he lifted his sandwich, I could see his veins rise up and do a ghostly glide over his knuckles. By the end of the day, I knew he had a talent for math and a weird Charles Dickens brand of morality. He said to me, "Everything you think—it's true. So think well." I could hardly imagine what he meant by that. My mind felt like an intractable claw. Every thought was a secret wish to be better than other people. But Noah, I found out, had a well-organized heart. A mind full of unusual, ambitious thoughts, which he daily cultivated and tended. All spring we walked home from school together, discussing his theories. He wondered whether we could live without the moon—if, say, a meteor scraped it surgically, and without harming the earth, from the sky. Was it ornament or necessary? What were ornaments? What were necessities? What was surgery? What was harm?

"We've gotten used to the moon," I said, by way of conclusion. "We can't give it up." Every once in a while, this could happen. A certain combination of words achieved by accident could make me feel expansive, luminous. Victorious.

He said, "Do we even look at it? Do we even care?"

"I don't *need* to look at it. I've *decided*."

"Don't get mad at me," he said.

"I'm not mad," I told him, furious. In fact, I didn't care one way or the other about the moon. I just wanted to seem smart. But Noah could always make any rhetorical victory of mine seem, at the last moment, unrelated to the real argument.

Our pattern was fixed when we got to his house. We each ate a bowl of Cheerios in silence, and then we went to his room where we took off our clothes, very careful not to mention—or even affect to notice—that this was what was happening. "Is this a new CD?" I'd ask. "Is that your sister's pen?" Once under the covers, we'd start discussing his theories again—ornaments versus necessities, a mooned versus a moonless world—and every time we touched it was as if by some extreme accident of circumstance. "Whoops!" Noah said once, as if he'd dropped a glass. A sprinkler blatted water against the window. There was a hand on my butt, a stuffed dog under my head, a face-shaped swirl of paint on the ceiling. Time crinkled up, got sticky. I can't remember

what we talked about then. All I can remember is my arm going
numb under the weight of his head, the leaking-sand sensation
of blood leaving my fingers. I remember the *click click* of saliva
breaking in his throat as he murmured in my ear. Then, after a
while, Noah would get another idea—a bigger catapult, a tauter
spring, a weapon we could build on wheels—and we'd dress in a
rush, grateful to be done with the strained, shameful drudgery of
coming up with things to say.

He wasn't a vampire, of course, but a Christian, a good one, so the
third catapult we built was a raft. We just kept adding things and
taking things off, until it was flat and huge and ready for water.
Noah's parents weren't sure they approved of this, so before we
tried it out they invited me to play Scrabble. They were white-
haired, tall, and looming people. Their white hair was incongruous
with their faces, which were unlined and playful, almost girlish.
They kept tickling each other as Noah distributed the wooden letters. Noah's little sister, Julie, arranged her pieces furtively under
the coffee table. In my corner of the couch, I smoldered in the
premature humiliation of defeat. I could feel my brain rising up in
a slow, inevitable panic; before I knew it, the letters were too far
away to be legible. I couldn't make out a word.

"Your turn," Noah's father said.

They watched me. It occurred to me then how bad my posture
was, my spine a curled hook. I had a crop of pimples on my forehead and a long purple bruise on my arm from shoving my brother
in a closet and forcing shut the door. I was still holding out hope
that my body could go back to being what it was a year ago, effortless and completely forgettable, but that was starting to seem less
and less likely. I tried to concentrate, but I didn't like how Noah's
family was looking at me so long, hoping so hard that I was sweet
and harmless and possibly Christian.

As they waited for me to finish my turn, Julie stood up and
played a few bars of Bach on the baby grand piano. As she played

with one hand, she leaned over to pet the dog with the other. "Dum, da-dum," she said.

"CERT," Noah's mother said to me, when I put my letters down. "Now, that's fine. Close enough, don't we think—" She looked around the room. "—to a real word."

Halfway through the game, Noah's father jumped up and said he had a book for me to borrow. He ran upstairs and bounded back down, setting the thing on my lap. He was an accountant, Noah had said, but his firm had let him go a few months back, and he'd since been spending a lot of time at the downtown library. "Just read the first page," he said. On the cover were rays of sun behind a man with outstretched arms. "Just read the first chapter."

"Here?" I asked.

"Just a few pages. There you go."

Now, sometimes, I think I can see the whole line of events that got me out of childhood—no event more or less important than the rest, just sequence, time doing its march—but then, I was always on a precipice. I was always balking. For instance, when Noah's father said, "Go ahead, read it," I felt his excitement like a menace, and I considered refusing. Why be what they wanted? Why read what he said? But I knew as well as anyone how to look like I was good, so I took the book and smiled it down.

An hour or so later, after the ice cream had been served and my dad had been called, Noah's father asked, "Did you make it to the end? What did you think?"

"Not quite. That man in the desert—"

"He wasn't exactly a man."

"The angel in the desert—"

"Katie, do you believe in God?"

I refused to meet his hopeful gaze. Instead, I fixed my eyes on the abandoned Scrabble board with its rows and columns of letters, and it seemed sad to me then, almost pathetic, that so much time should be wasted on words that told no message and made no story. It was all just points.

"Sometimes, maybe," I said, because Noah's father was waiting for an answer and there wasn't any other way out. But I sliced my words down the middle into two equal pieces. The meaning said, "Maybe," and the tone said this: "A nice person would fuck off, and you, I guess, are not a nice person."

The raft we built was wonderful, a great big flying saucer of plywood and two-by-fours, which we fastened together with screws and nails and set in the creek. It was high summer by then, and we knew we could float for miles before the creek hit the waterfall and fell, near Fort Snelling, into the Mississippi. We floated lazily through the suburban backyards of the city, startling children on their swing sets and fathers at their smoky grills. We used canoe paddles to get us through the rapids. Once, we were overtaken by a swarm of sleek plastic kayaks that shot like bullets through the water. In our raft, we sat cross-legged on life jackets, let the currents curl us around and around. We were happy. We got stuck in cattails and tree roots. When the creek widened out, we lay on our backs and let the sun burn us. We were past sunscreen—we were way past all that. We floated feet-first under low-hanging bridges, through golf courses and under highways, past the penitentiary with its barbed-wire coils. The prisoners playing basketball were surprised to see us, and one of them rushed the fence and pretended to climb it, as if we could help row him an escape from jail. "No! Stay there!" Noah waved him down, laughing. "We'll come back! We'll come back for you later!"

Once, a red-winged blackbird dropped onto Noah's cap, balanced there for a moment, and then seemed to slide through the air onto a nearby cattail.

Once, a boy barreling down the creek path on a skateboard raced us to the next bridge, then spat a wad of gum that landed on my paddle. The gum clung to the wood like a gray, wrinkly leech. "Grow up!" Noah yelled at him, and the boy, who was maybe twelve, said, "I'm not the one on a shitty old board in the creek. *You* grow up!"

Late in the day my dad showed up, waving at us as we floated under a bicycle-path bridge near Lake Nokomis. He didn't say anything. He just stood with one hand in the air until we waved back, and then he set both hands on the railing and watched as we were sucked out of sight in the current under the bridge.

"What's he doing here?" Noah whispered as we ducked under the wood planks. "How'd he find us?"

"I don't know," I whispered back. "I told him we'd be on the creek today. He's probably just checking in, making sure we haven't drowned."

Overhead, my father was wheeling his three-speed bike across the bridge and back to the road. I could hear the low rumbling of the planks, the creaking adjustments and readjustments to his weight. I hoped he'd just go home. I knew he worried about me— for years, I'd spent too much time in the woods, watched too little TV—but I thought he seemed reassured now that I was spending so many of my days with Noah. A teenage girl with a boyfriend is, if nothing else, normal.

Noah lifted his paddle up and thudded it against a concrete piling. "He's checking in with *you*, you mean."

"What's the difference?"

"He doesn't trust me. He thinks I'm making you into a Christian or something."

I rolled my eyes. "He doesn't even *know* you're a Christian."

He paused, put his paddle on his lap. "Why not?"

"What do you mean, why not?"

When Noah was annoyed, he would smooth his voice down flat. No landmarks, no intonation. "You know what I mean. Are you embarrassed by it or something? You know what I mean."

Did I? Here again was the old temptation: the desire to prove something to him, to win, which would be the same as losing a different, more obscure argument. But I couldn't help myself. I did in fact know what he meant, or thought I did, and I wanted him to feel bad for speaking to me as if we weren't on the raft—as if we were still in his house, or in his bed. I felt betrayed. "It's not important to me," I said, as the raft surged through the water and spit us out into the light. "I don't care about it at all. I never think about it, that's why I didn't tell my dad. Who cares?"

After the raft sank and couldn't be repaired, we sat around for a few days with his sister at the park. Julie was a burgeoning athlete. She always had a tennis racket or a baseball bat, a muscle set that needed toning. Sometimes we could talk the neighborhood boys into letting her in a soccer game, and then we'd go back to Noah's empty house and draw up plans for our time machine. By July, Noah's bed was hot, a wrinkled coil of sheets that kept us turning from our bellies to our backs, from our backs to our bellies. We moved like stones in waves, like sunbathers. We didn't call it a time machine, of course. The title we put on the tab of our manila folder after we got dressed was: A Hypothesis for Quantum Tunneling. What I liked best was the library where we went after lunch because it was air-conditioned and mostly empty, just mothers with mottled babies in slings and sleeping homeless people. The books we read had been read by someone else, someone who folded the pages down and wrote in pencil little marginal notes like, *the problem of the grandfather paradox.* "I don't know if this guy understood any of this," Noah said, excited. As he read, he scraped curled bits of wood from his pencil tip with a fingernail. "There's a whole fourth dimension you can't see with anything but math."

For Noah, this made the time machine better than the catapult or the raft. It was so much more inviolable and ambitious.

He forbade me from using the run-of-the-mill language of "moving" or "traveling" in time, and instead insisted on talking exclusively of world lines and closed time-like curves, in which, Noah said, an event can be simultaneous with its cause, and may be able to cause itself. "This is something most people don't think about at all," Noah pointed out. It was hard for me to tell how serious Noah really was about this project. Sometimes it seemed as though we were mocking the people who believed this stuff, like the guy with the marginal note that said p*lace - time = memory - mind.* ("How lame," Noah said. "How completely dumb.") And other times it seemed we were mocking them because they didn't believe it enough—weren't determined and talented enough to take it seriously.

One afternoon, I talked Noah into checking out our books from the library and walking to the 7-Eleven. We sat on the sidewalk outside, stabbing tunnels in red slush with our straws. "Can I have a sip of yours?" I asked. I wanted to put my mouth where Noah's mouth was, I wanted him to see my throat working.

But he was already standing up.

"I've got an idea," he said. "You want to hear what I'm thinking about?"

I didn't really. I was getting a little bored of relativity, and so I dawdled as we crossed the street, let a car get too close and honk at me. I gave the driver—a pregnant lady rubbing her belly—the finger. Her expression was unruffled, almost smug, as if she expected this from me, as if I was just some punk teenager like all the others. Then I wanted to hold up my book, *General Relativity in the Age of Allegory*, in my defense. I wanted to show her what her bullied, ordinary mind could not begin to comprehend. I wanted to make time twist into a miraculous disastrous tunnel and take its own tail in its mouth—*ouroboros, wormy Death Hole, formula for stasis, the nourishment of God*—but the instant the words appeared, then disappeared, from my head, I tucked the book under my arm so she couldn't see it as she passed. "Come on," Noah called, but I was incensed at him suddenly and shouted back, "Did you even look for traffic before you stepped into the road? What the hell's wrong with you?"

He gave me a look like I'd kicked him.

For the moment, I didn't care about hurting him. The problem was it was getting harder for me to tell if I was far, far ahead of everyone else—or somehow behind other kids my age, the ones who spent their days at the pool and at Taco Bell.

I grew ashamed, a little secretive. One night, Ashley Leber from across the street called to ask if I could take over a babysitting job. When I made an excuse about being too busy, she said she'd heard I built a boat with Noah and took it to the creek—"Noah's Ark," she called it. "Are you still dating that Evangelical freak?" she asked. "Excuse my language."

"No," I said. "Not really."

"Not that *you'd* be a freak for dating him. He's hot."

"Yeah," I said. "I guess."

The thing was, I used to spend a lot of time with those girls, Ashley and her friends, who lived on my block. There were summers when we basically lived in our backyards, scrambling over the chain link fences. Now those same girls rode their ten-speed bikes down the sidewalks to the mall, where they ate samples of frozen yogurt from doll-sized spoons. "You can eat as much as you want," Ashley told me from her bike one day, "and it's all free, and you don't get fat."

At some point in the last year, they'd started treating me with an evasive respect, like someone's frail grandma. Like someone who'd taken care of them once, and now was to be humored. It was true, in a way. When we were eleven, twelve, I'd taken care of them all. Summer evenings, I used to usher them into the woods to play in the stand of old pines behind our houses. In the deep shade of the trees, I'd quieted them down. I'd taken their shoes from them, and I'd taken their socks. I'd made their wimpy girl fantasies into categorical facts. I told them where to stand, how to walk, how to do the stories. *Look, the club-footed horse thief made you lame so you'd have to make love to him. Limp, limp. Look, the limping princess tried to escape on a horse stolen from the thief's stable. You, gallop. You, stop. Put your heart into it.* I don't remember Ashley, in particular, being there with us. There were only believers and doubters: I saw no other distinctions, considered none of them friends. You either believed what the mind could do—and took your severed horse hoof and found what solace there was—or you didn't, and were a kid. I had no patience for pretenders, for people who needed shoes or snacks. I converted them all. They loved me because I was the only one who could get them through it, past their own marginal, limited minds, which required so many little suicides, so much constant sacrifice, surrender after surrender.

So when Ashley rolled up that day on her bike, I could honestly say I didn't feel anything for her. She was nobody. A girl with a plastic hair-clip in her mouth, like a bit. Junior high had changed everything between us. I didn't need her to stop her bike and ask me with such strained deference to come along, as if I'd ever needed something from her. "There's a flavor with gum in it," she said to me, still hesitating at my driveway.

"Okay," I said. But when she started a smile by pulling her hair by the roots into a ponytail, I added, "I've got stuff to do though. This project I'm working on."

She shrugged and made a lopsided ponytail with one hand. Rode on.

The project was going poorly, however. Noah's parents got worried that we were spending too much time alone, so they started calling him during the day when they were gone. By late July they were taking turns, calling every hour, on the hour. His mother called from her desk at church and his father called from gas stations where he lunched on hotdogs. He was meeting contacts in the field, Noah said, looking for a job that let him be himself, which, I guess, meant not getting punished for speculating about angels. In the kitchen, Noah would wind the phone cord around his neck, like a noose, and politely reassure him. "Julie's at the neighbor's. She's fine. I'm fine. The house keeps on not burning down."

More and more now, we stayed at the table with our books after cereal. Noah was getting impatient with our progress on a propulsion system for time dilation. He seemed harried by the numbers, stressed out. He didn't have time for taking the dog out, so I did that, and other chores too, like filling the dishwasher. At the table, Noah took notes on his father's legal pads, and when there was nothing else for me to do, I made doodles next to his notes. I drew rafts and vessels and boats, anything that could float away.

Once, the phone rang when Noah was in the middle of a troubling equation. He had his head in both hands, and I could see him squeezing his skull, the blue veins riding over his knuckles. His veins were like a second, more complicated hand that lived inside the ordinary one. He groaned. "Answer that, please? I'm working on something."

I stood up at once, feeling the complete uselessness of my limbs, which I could not arrange in a tidy, concentrated hunch over math the way Noah did. I was always crouching in my chair, pulling out a single strand of hair and setting it adrift in the sunshine with the dust.

"Well!" It was Noah's dad on the phone. He sounded startled, as if someone had come up from behind and said *boo*. "It's nice to get you on the phone, Katie. What are you up to today?"

"Not much."

"Okay. Well. Listen." He had nothing else to say, and in the wake of his last word I heard him change the phone to his other ear. I could actually hear his stubble scrape against the mouthpiece.

"Is there something I should tell Noah?"

"Tell him I'll be home at six?" He made it into a question. What he really wanted to know was something else, something only I could tell him.

But I felt no responsibility to reassure Noah's dad, who hadn't let me go home until I'd skimmed through his whole book about a man who walked barefoot across the Sahara, who lay down and almost died of dehydration, and then got back up again when an angel arrived on a cloud. That man was a moron, a liar. His story wasn't convincing at all. "No problem!" I told Noah's dad now, egging him on a little because I knew I could. "I'll let Noah know. He's waiting for me, so I should get back to him. You won't be here for, what, like another five hours? No worries! We'll figure out *something* to do until Julie gets home."

The next day, Julie came home earlier than usual, and I put together a lunch for her that was three slices of cheese and a Popsicle on a plate. We went into the backyard so she could drip if she needed to. I noticed she had grass stains on her knees from a rough game of soccer and dried sweat under her ears. When she finished her Popsicle, she slid the whole stick in her mouth, like a knife eater, and then spat it hard across the yard. The dog took off after it.

"My dad said not to play at the park for more than an hour, which isn't long enough for a real game if anyone's any good." She looked at me suspiciously. "What are you and Noah doing with all those books, anyway? Studying for the SATs or something?"

She arched her body backward into a bridge as she said this, and began to inch around—her face going red, her honey-brown hair whisking the grass. For a moment, she reminded me of my girls in the woods, the best ones, who refused to give the excuse of their bodies. Those girls climbed two stories up a pine tree when I told them. They hung upside down from legs like hooks.

"It's not schoolwork," I said. I didn't want her to think I was some kind of nerd, to confuse me with the kids who were always worrying about getting into a good college.

She pulled out of her bridge and lay flat in the grass. "Well, what?"

I decided to try the truth on her. She was back in her bridge before I said a word, and I thought, as she scuttled around with her shirt slipping over her head, she might understand. Her nipples faced me like eyes. "It's hard to explain," I sighed. "It's pretty complicated, but it's not about schoolwork. We don't care about college. We're working on something called a quantum tunnel." Julie sat down on the grass, hard, and because she didn't seem impressed at all, I added, "That's like a time machine."

"Noah's building a time machine?"

"And *I* am."

I could tell by her posture she was wary. She was afraid I wasn't taking her seriously, that I was mocking her because she was ten and I had nothing else to do with my time. She said, picking up a leaf and tearing it to bits, "Is that even possible?"

"Well, it seems theoretically possible to travel," I wasn't supposed to use that word, "to *tunnel* into the future. But not the past. Nobody seems to agree about the past. But most everyone thinks you could go to the future."

"You're going to the future?" The way she said this—so slowly, a piece of leaf in her mouth—I could tell she was now considering it for real. I wanted very much, then, to crouch over and whisper in her ear, to convince her. Little girls are so pliable. It would be nothing, it would be like knocking over a full glass of water, to get her to believe me.

But then she bloomed back into her bridge and walked on her backward-facing palms over to the driveway. "Aren't we going to the future already? What kind of time machine is that? What we already do."

She had a point, and I felt my fingers go stiff on my lap. Then I reminded myself: Julie never did have any real talent for making things up. "Well, the theory is it gets us there *faster*." I stood up. "Spit that leaf out of your mouth, okay? That's gross."

Noah began to give up hope in August. He'd been so sure we'd come to a conclusion one way or another by the end of the summer, but it seemed we were getting further and further away from a tenable theory rather than closer and closer. He kept trying to understand math that made him set his head on his book and groan. "We'll need a course in calculus," he moaned one afternoon. "We'll need to go to college, maybe graduate school. I kept thinking we could just skip over derivatives, but now I think we can't." He lifted his head and there was a welt on his cheek from where the book's staircase of pages had marked him.

We ate cereal and watched the dog pee under the deck because it was raining. "Where's Julie?" Noah wondered, looking worried for once, as if she had just occurred to him for the first time all summer. We went and stood in the open threshold of the sliding glass door, where we could feel the displacement of air from the rain.

"I don't know," I said. "She's *your* sister."

Anything could wound him. Which was one of the reasons I loved him, I guess, and why I knew I would stick around for longer than made sense, maybe marry him. He sat down morosely on the planks of the stairs, let the rain drench him.

I said—sorry now, soothing him—"You're getting soaked. Come back inside."

"It doesn't matter."

"You look like a bad movie, seriously. There should be music so we can just sit and watch you and feel sad."

He started humming a song I didn't know, then stopped. "You know what?" He laughed in a way that didn't sound like laughing. "My parents think we're *doing it*." He rubbed the rain off the face of his watch and gave it a heartbreaking look.

Right on cue, the phone started ringing. Between each ring, the silence went on and on, and I was sure, each time, that that was the end. And then, each time, it rang again.

"*Doing* it?" I laughed at his wording. "What in the *world* makes them think that?"

He stood up. "Let's go inside. I don't want to talk about it."

Neither did I. We lay damply in his bed in silence. No small talk, for once, and no planning. At first I found the silence inordinately exciting. We lay naked on our backs without touching, and my knees felt welded together with sweat. Without any talk to distract us, even my breathing felt enormous, wicked enough to disturb the bed as air went in and out of my chest. It occurred to me in a way it never had before that if he looked over at me, even once, he would see everything. I breathed, and held my breath. Breathed.

But then I realized Noah was only silent because he was depressed. I felt his misery moving off him in immobilizing waves.

"Noah," I said. "We could build another raft. We could do something else."

"It's not that. I don't care if we build anything. I just want to know whether it's possible, you know? So we haven't wasted all this time on nothing. It doesn't have to *actually* happen."

The phone started up again, and between each ring, I waited.

But neither of us got out of bed.

After a moment, I took his hand and starting talking. I didn't know what I was talking about. I was telling stories, bullshitting, making things up, but mostly I was just hoping Noah would shift his shoulder into my breast and pretend it hadn't happened. I was hoping if I talked long enough about something else, we could pretend I wasn't taking his dick in my hand like an animal I'd caught by simply bending down and opening up my fingers.

There would be no time machine, of course, but we didn't say that.

I never told Noah about my girls in the woods, though I wish I had. They hung upside down from branches, and I watched their heads fill up, one by one, with blood. I stood on the ground and let them dangle. "I'm sick," some of them pleaded. "Let me come down." And I did. But the best ones stayed and were bats, vampires. They crossed their wrists over their chests, and they didn't fall. They said they would fall, they said their legs were getting tired. They said there was a ringing in their ears (a music, I told them, a song for crisis), but they just kept on shining in the tree like Christmas decorations. Human flags. I didn't tell Noah, but if I had, I would have explained that they didn't fall, not one of them.

The strange thing about that woods when I think back on it is that it was just Mr. Ferter's untended backyard, with rolls of chicken wire beneath buckthorn and a bunch of rusty lawnmowers. I remember I had a stick that was twice as tall as I was. I hoisted it over my head—majestically, I felt—and in this way, I could touch those beet-red dangling hands (the ones who couldn't keep them crossed over their chests) and stir all that brackish hair. I could tap the bug-eyed nipples on their chests when they let their arms go and their shirts bunched up around their armpits. Even now I remember how good that felt. I felt everything as if the twigged point of the stick were my own fingertip, which was precise but so unwieldy as well, so tricky to manage. Nobody ever really appreciated that. The skill.

Just before school started, Noah's parents started making him go in twice a week for private talks with his minister. The first thing this minister did was forbid him to be alone in the house with his girlfriend. This wasn't much of an obstacle, though, because Noah could say with complete truthfulness that he and I had never even discussed having any kind of romantic relationship. Later, his minister revised his earlier recommendation and warned Noah not to spend time alone at home with a girl who did not share his moral values and his most sacred beliefs. "I told him we have lots of projects together, but he said I won't find peace." Noah looked hunched over and old when he told me. In keeping with the minister's rules, we were sitting in his driveway. "He said I will never be happy that way."

"Are you happy *now?*" We had the catapult out and had rigged up a system that smashed Lego man straight into the cement.

I shouldn't have asked it. The dog came out of the garden and scooped up Lego man with his mouth. Noah clapped his hands and ran after him. "*Leave* it!" he howled. He pried open the dog's face and wrenched Lego man free from its jaws. "*Bad* dog. Shame."

He came back, set a glistening Lego man in his Dixie cup, and I wondered then what it was like to be a real Christian, to live inside that shut box, to live with all those corners and walls, and way up at the top, just one little shuttered window.

"Noah," I said to him. "What would happen if we *could* go to the future? Just skip over all this, and, ta-da, be twenty-four or sixty-two?"

He was a child now. He was a boy throwing rocks at a dog. He didn't want to play this game. "I don't know."

I tried another tack. "Or what if you were, like, born without limbs. Without arms and without legs. Could you be content?"

"That doesn't make sense." But he sat down to think about it. He pulled the lever and sent Lego man skidding across the cement on his chest. "Maybe. Maybe in certain circumstances."

"Or what if a meteor came and scraped Earth from the solar system? Whack. Would God be sad?"

"He would and he wouldn't. The earth is just an idea that God has, I think. A thought in His mind, which can't actually be—"

"Be?"

"I'm trying to think of the word. Changed. Damaged."

The dog skidded out from behind a bush, scooped up Lego man in his mouth, and ran off toward the creek. It was strange how satisfying that was, how glad I was to be done, finally, with the catapult game, and I told Noah in a rush that I was willing to believe the possibility that God existed.

He shook his head. "You *don't* believe in God."

"Sure, I do," I said as an experiment. I imagined the face I'd have to wear as a Christian, the knowing half smile that you see in Jesus pictures, as if swallowing something dangerous without moving your lips. I thought, if I tried, I could learn to play the piano and be a generous but talented Scrabble player. I could have better posture. I'd convinced people of far stranger things. I had been one-legged, lame, a beetle, a murderer. I'd made children into bats.

He could have tested me. He could have pursued it so much further than that. But that was enough for him. "Come on," he said, standing up. "I'm hungry."

Inside we stirred cereal in cloudy milk and tossed the last soggy pieces to the dog. Then we lay the wrong way in Noah's bed, our heads hanging off one end and our feet hanging off the other. Over us, the people in the ceiling paint seemed unable to close their mouths; I could feel the ache that was the ache of their faces. Noah wanted to talk about timetables for the universe, but I had decided to act the good Christian—to be better, so much better than he was at this—and I wouldn't let him touch me, even by accident. We were naked, as usual, but I kept my body out of reach.

When he put his hand on my breast, I said, innocent as Adam's dust, "What are you doing, Noah?"

He barely blinked. He took his hand back and said, "Okay, here's the thing. I know it seems like a dead end, but I've been considering cosmological horizons as an important part of the Big Bang space-time, which undermines our understanding of what can be observed in the past. As well as, I guess, our ability to influence future events."

"Stop that," I said, playing Good. I sounded uncertain, I thought, which was an acceptable way for a Good Christian to sound, given the circumstances.

He thumbed my nipple just once, so I said—as if sad, as if completely worn down—"Noah? Do you want to have sex?"

He was quiet for a moment. "No," he finally said. "All I'm trying to say is that—" He lifted his head up, took a breath, and when he spoke again he was whining. "I want to go back to what I was saying."

He put the backs of his hands over his eyes, dug his knuckles in. Our heads were still hanging off the bed, and I saw that his face had long ago filled with blood, a flush that made the veins in his forehead visible. Close as I was, I could see a dozen or more tiny lines, like cracks, all purple and branching scalpward.

That's when my plan changed slightly. That's when I saw that what we did and what we said were two different things, two sides of a wheel that went around and around and would never meet. So I took his dick in my hand and I squeezed it, gently, in rhythm with his words, which meant nothing. He seemed to like that. Then for a moment his words were the important part—he was describing the transparent nature of the universe after its opaque start—and what I did with my hand was completely insignificant, far too trivial for notice, something children did because they hadn't yet learned any better. "No, wait," he said once, but by then the wheel had gone around again and I wasn't listening to him anymore. I sat up, the world swinging to black as blood rushed from my head, and I climbed on top of him. I felt something like a stripe of pain painted down my gut, that's all. He jerked away once and gave in. He wouldn't look at me then, and I must have been crying because a strand of snot dangled from my nose. I leaned down over him to wipe it off. I meant to tell him when we were done with this, *Listen, when we're done with this*, we could say whatever we wanted. We could say I was a Christian. We could say he was a virgin. We could go back to the past. But then the phone started ringing, and instead of saying this out loud, I crouched there over him, awkwardly, holding my dripping nose, waiting for the ringing to stop.

ONE YOU RUN FROM, THE OTHER YOU FIGHT

Nora sat on the balcony after dinner and wrote out checks. "It'll be easy," Sage promised. "We'll zip around and eat cheeses." But Nora felt a flush of dread. She didn't like these events, the ritual fawning over other people's children.

It was late spring and the mosquitoes were descending. One landed on her arm, and Nora watched it part the fine hairs and look around. It had a face like an important utensil.

"Whinnie McPhire!" Sage cried, reading the name off the invitation. "What can you possibly say to a teenager named that?"

Whinnie McPhire lived in the nice part of town where the trees were a hundred years old and, therefore, diseased. In front of the house there was a white oak with a tire swing and a bulbous growth like an engorged doorknob. A bluish dog ran to the curb and stopped abruptly, spinning idiot circles on its hind legs. Nora stooped and put her hand out, but Sage said, "It's an electric fence. One more step and bzzzt!"

He giggled. Sage was scornful of money, thought himself better than their friends who sought it, and loved an opportunity to deride them. He couldn't keep the excitement out of his voice. He said, "Ready for Miss Class of 2009?"

Inside, they were ushered straight from the door to the food: card tables draped in green plastic and folds of turkey on trays. There was a blown-up portrait of the graduate hanging from the ceiling, her blonde head floating over the olives. Nora looked for the girl's mother, an old friend from college, but she was nowhere around. Everyone stood with green paper plates and plastic knives, eating and talking and touching their teeth for seeds. A man near the cheese dip asked Nora and Sage how long they'd been together. Sage clapped the man's arm. He said, "Old man, too long, too long," and the man, not understanding Sage's tone, laughed with him. The man said, "I hear divorce can do great things for a marriage!"

Nora pulled the pit of an olive from her mouth. "We're not married."

They got lost on their way to the second one, Nora driving, Sage telling her to count the blocks. "It's a grid," he said. "It goes either up or down." They found it because there was a rented rickshaw outside, teenage boys with long dyed hair dragging teenage girls. This one had a Chinese theme, with paper lanterns and cream cheese puffs. Inexplicably, the graduate wore a bow tie and a top hat. "He's *artsy*," a little woman whispered to Nora, as the graduate did a spinning trick with his cane. Everyone applauded, and then his mother and father climbed into a dragon costume, one at the head and one at the tail.

In the car again, Sage kissed her. "I thought I was going to have to take that thing by the nose and guide it into traffic." He rolled his window down and draped his hand out, humming. He was thrilled. Nora let the car move under her. They'd been together for nine years, and she knew how much of their relationship depended on shared contempt. Pity the sellouts. Pity the spoiled children, the lonely husbands and nervous wives. Nora and Sage held part-time teaching jobs and kept themselves respectable.

"It's beautiful out here," Nora said, "isn't it?" They were driving into the part of the suburb where a few old farms remained, wedged between the subdivisions.

"People don't give *near* enough credit to suburban sprawl." Sage nodded. "It makes all the ugly farms that ruined the prairie look so much better. Like Bush the first. Bring in the son, and we grow wistful for the father."

Sage had severe dyslexia as a child and retained an odd habit of turning his head and looking at faraway things from the corner of his eye. This made his face seem dubious and scheming; people had difficulty trusting him. They felt he was hiding something, and Sage, in turn, felt rebuffed. Nora, though, was fond of his sideways glance. It meant he was paying close attention.

She said, smiling a little, "What I miss is the swamp."

He said, "I miss the town dump. Do you remember? Any old clearing in the forest, and in goes the broke-down refrigerator. Leaky batteries. Old books and comics, even encyclopedias!"

They were driving more slowly now. Overhead, the clouds were white and tall, like shoveled drifts of snow.

Nora said, abruptly, "I found a tarot card once."

"In a dump?"

"In a student paper."

She wasn't sure what made her think of this. It happened a long time ago, back when she was barely older than her students. For years she thought of that period in her life as The Mistake, when she was dating a yogi and had joined a macrobiotics club. Now that just felt like someone else's tedious story.

In the passenger seat, Sage was trying to get another envelope out of the glove compartment. "Someone had a crush on you."

"It wasn't that kind of tarot card." She pulled into a driveway with two rusted station wagons. "It was a horned man with a blindfold."

"The devil!" Sage cried. "You must have really pissed off the kid who left it for you. Did you give him a bad grade?"

"I don't remember."

But she did. The boy sucked lemon drops and his nipples showed through his shirt and she gave him an F even though he killed himself before she could get the paper back to him. Or maybe that was someone else. Maybe she was confusing things.

Sage started opening the door, but Nora called, "Wait!"

She wanted to tell him something. She had the impulse to be comforted, so she leaned over the seat and put her head on his lap. Then Nora thought about the dream she had, the one where Sage was pregnant with their baby. He was a big man, and he let the baby grow into a small child in his womb—a big, toddler-sized fetus. Sage grew fat and Nora stayed thin. In the dream she felt forgiven.

Sage licked the envelope over her and patted her head. Nora could smell the bright, sticky scent of glue and wet paper.

The screen door was propped open with the statue of a frog, but the inner wooden door was shut and Sage had to jiggle the knob. Inside, they saw a few blue plastic cups on the coffee table. There were potted flowers instead of florist arrangements, petunias drooping from window sills.

"Where's the prodigy?" Sage sang out. But when no one answered, he said, more hesitantly, "Hello?"

There was a collection of soccer trophies on the mantelpiece, little bronze boys balancing balls on their shoes. In the middle of the crowd was a candid photo, a kid in dark sunglasses turning his head.

Sage looked at Nora. "Did we get the right time?"

She could feel him shrinking back, closing down. Sage didn't like to feel socially vulnerable. She said, "It's an open house. There is no right time."

"Well, did we get the right day?"

"Agda!" Nora called into the kitchen. Then she turned to Sage and whispered, "Or is it Inga?" She muttered, "It's some funny Swedish name."

Sage said, "Allie?"

"That's not Swedish."

Sage was backing up. "We should go."

Nora rolled her eyes at him. It was perverse of her, but she liked it when Sage was thrown off by unexpected events. He grew shy and suspicious; he didn't know whom to disparage and whom to defend. It was understood, then, that Nora was the sensible one, the one to defer to. She said, officiously, "We should check upstairs."

"God, Nora. No. No way. That's like breaking and entering."

"We were invited. We should make sure nothing's wrong."

Nora climbed the stairs gingerly, but without hesitation. She noticed the bedroom walls were gray with fingerprints. On the bed, the covers were pushed to one side as if love or sleep had only recently ended.

Sage declared anxiously from behind her, "Not a burglary. Nothing taken."

Nora hushed him. "How would *you* know if anything's gone?"

She touched a slippery doorknob. She wanted to see what the Svensons kept in their closets: the puckery blue condoms, the drafts of unfinished poems. Nora believed that everyone had things they wanted seen but couldn't show, things they did poorly for which they wanted to be absolved. It made her feel perceptive and benevolent to realize this about the Svensons, who were dowdy and boring to talk to. Very gently, she pulled open the closet door.

"Stop it!" Sage pushed the door closed. He had a slightly hounded look, like something was biting at his neck under his shirt. "Enough of this. We'll just leave the card on the table and go."

But the boy's bedroom! Nora paused in the doorway and looked in. There was a neatly made bed, a poster of a giant hand flicking someone off, and an aquarium. She walked over and crouched by the glass. Teenage boys always unnerved her, with their dramatic bodies and bad skin, their needy flirtation. They couldn't decide if they wanted to be liked or hated. The student with the lemon drops used to pull them out of his mouth and line them up, glistening and almost beautiful, on his desk. She remembered that he wrote eleven drafts of one paper, each with fewer and fewer pages until he was left with a single sentence: *Doesthisimpressyourhighness?* Inside the aquarium, a fluorescent light buzzed over waxy plants. Nora didn't see anything alive in there, and then several unrelated stones clicked together and became a millipede.

Nora jumped back.

Sage, already on the stairs, called, "Did you hear something?"

She met him in the hall.

He said, hopefully, "Someone's home?"

They walked down the stairs together, neither one leading or following, like a bride and a groom at a wedding. Nora had the impression people were hiding, friends stashed behind doorways and chairs. She thought the guest of honor at a surprise party might feel something like this before the lights flicked on, and she almost took Sage's hand, almost warned him to pay attention. But the living room was just as they left it, the same bronze boys kicking daintily in unison. The kitchen, too, was unremarkable. Ragged cereal boxes on the counter and half-empty coffee mugs. Nora had the impulse to dip her finger in one of them to see if the liquid was still warm.

She gave a start when she saw it, but the bear didn't bother to lift its head.

When she thought about that afternoon later, it worried Nora that she couldn't reconstruct her logic. She just remembered how relieved she felt in that moment, the weight of everything lifted off with the sheer unlikeliness of the danger. Her mind raced with stories: bears rolling tents over, campers jumping off cliffs to escape. She whispered to Sage, "Is it brown or black?" because she'd heard one you run from and the other you fight, but the bear looked too scrawny to be dangerous, ancient and sluggish, something only slightly more animated than an eroded boulder. It hovered over two white plates on the floor, clean enough to pile up and return to the cabinets. Then the animal took a step forward and Nora had the presence of mind to throw a box of cereal. Sage said, "What the fuck!" and the cereal box hit a cabinet with a thud. The bear gave them a pathetic, desperate look—ears back and tail between its legs—and Nora noticed it was in fact a dog. It was difficult to see because the sun was setting so brilliantly. The globe of light slid into the frame of the window and distracted them all for an instant; it was so unnecessary, so blinding. Then the dog shrugged to the floor and lifted one leg in the air, peeing and nibbling Chex at the same time.

"What's *wrong* with you?" Sage asked. "For Christ's sake."

Nora opened her mouth but didn't say anything. The important thing, she knew, was to accuse him first, for not seeing the bear for even a second, for not perceiving even a little bit of danger. Her fingers hung from her hands (she felt them dangling wetly there, one by one) and she was furious then because she could not even mention the bear without feeling ashamed.

"Oh my God," Sage muttered. "The thing peed itself."

He went to a cupboard and opened a door, closed it and opened another.

"What are you doing?" Her voice was very high and ringing.

"Looking for some paper towels."

"Where *are* we?" she demanded.

"Nora, calm down. You're freaking the dog out."

"No really! Who's *house* is this?" she asked, in horror.

It was absurd to see Sage so practical and generous all of a sudden. He was kneeling down and petting the dog, pushing the hair out if its eyes, murmuring softly. Since when did he know what to do with pets, how to comfort them? The dog was one of those hideous, otherworldly mixes with ears that rose partway and collapsed, with gray paw pads like the skins of old fruits. Nora wanted the bear back.

The animal sat up and caught Sage's face with its tongue, drumming its tail on the kitchen floor.

She said, "That's disgusting."

He didn't say anything.

"You're disgusting." She was humiliated.

He stood up to wet the paper towels, but she took the roll from him. She could never just leave him alone, could never quite solace herself adequately. "You like wiping pee, Sage?"

"Fuck off."

"Later, you can stroke my brow and wipe my ass, if you want, like the doggy."

He shoved away the paper she held for the job. The windows were getting dark, and the kitchen smelled like wet animal. The bear had been shaggy, Nora remembered. Hulking and quiet, maybe injured. In the sink, she saw bloated peas drift in greasy water. Soon, someone would come home and be frightened. Nora and Sage would frighten them. They left before anyone came.

A small crowd gathered in front of the next house, a man waving smoke from his face at a grill, a clump of teenagers sipping sodas. As they walked up the driveway, a woman spotted them and said, "Are you cocktail-frank people, or sausage-ball?" Later, they drank wine from clear plastic glasses and watched a video of a girl they did not know riding a horse around and around a dusty field. Nora told jokes about herself to a teenager in shorts who wanted to flirt with her. "I drove a boy like you to suicide," she said, when it had grown late and parents and children alike were draped over furniture. She liked that it came out like a way to tease someone and not like an excuse for herself.

"You're bad."

She assured him, "I'm worse than I look."

He had his head on the back of the couch, very near her shoulder. "You don't *look* bad."

With effort she laughed at him. She saw Sage in the other room, touching the stubble on his face with the very tips of his fingers. He wouldn't catch her eye. The boy on the couch rearranged his shorts and waited for her to stop laughing.

"You don't know me." She resumed flirting.

"What does that have to do with anything?"

It was very late when they left. Sage was driving, fiddling with the radio. Nora felt the suburbs move past, dark and spectral. She wanted to reach out and touch Sage's hand, but that seemed too complicated. "Watch out for deer," she told him instead. She said it again when he didn't respond. Then she was crying. She thought about how once, years ago when they were making love, she hit her head on Sage's knee. Bright white lights had unfurled in her right eye. He had leaned over her in the dark, had kissed her face over and over again. "I'm sorry, I'm sorry, I'm sorry," he'd murmured, as if those were the only words of love in the world.

"Watch out," she told him now, but it didn't sound like love.

MARCO POLO

Before I go to sleep, I make the bed. I like that neat square: all the corners lined up, all the corners folded over each other. Sheets, blanket, comforter, pillowcase. For five minutes, I lie on top, then slowly crawl under, upsetting everything.

No one ever makes the bed in the morning. The rumpled landscape stays—hills, plateaus, valleys—casting bewitching shadows in the afternoon. Sometimes, I think the shape holds the shapes of our bodies, sleeping. But mostly, I think it holds the shape of our bodies leaving, the places where a head lifted up, a leg slid out, a person rose. I'm always gone before A in the morning. I don't know how she wakes up. But at night when I smooth down her sheets, I find myself imagining how she might transition out of her sleep. Once in a Minnesota lake, she hid from me for a full minute under the flat, black surface. She came out without explanation, clambered onto the dock and toweled dry. I think her waking must be like that—abrupt, but efficient.

I think, too, about how she should find my body when she finally comes to bed. Should I be on my back like an untroubled man? I could be like that, practical about my circadian rhythms.

It's just sleep, after all. Or should I be found coiled up, twisted in sheets, sweaty with dreams, with waiting? Would she be sorry then? Would she come to me from her side of the bed, would she put her arms around me? While I exchange one position for the next, night comes down on top of me. It bears down on me, so I can't move, so I can no longer consider my options. I don't ever know how she finds me. If I wake at all, it's usually too late for the traffic outside, too late for the TV in the neighboring apartment, too late for the dogs calling out against the sirens.

And A is in my arms, curled effortlessly against me.

She tells me I'm a lunatic, it's not like she's having an affair. I think that's probably true. She's never been good at subtlety or deception. When we were first married, she came to bed with me every night, settled her naked body on top of mine, settled her face in my neck. I could tell she liked it, but she wasn't romantic in the least. She arranged her breasts on my ribs and said, "Watch where you stick that knee." After I covered her face with kisses, she nodded approvingly, saying, "That's it, there we go." Then she put her head down and went to work. It was only afterward, when she was pulling her hair from my mouth, that she grew conversational. That's when she wanted to tell me the names of horses she rode as a child. She wanted to talk about China.

But she never wanted to fall asleep. Sometimes she waited until I drifted off before creeping out, fumbling for her shirt and socks, slipping through the door. I'd wake when she sat up and watch her prepare to go, shaking her hair loose from her collar. Sometimes, she just tucked me under the sheet, kissed my head, and left, hauling her clothes after her. In the morning, she was nonchalant. When asked, she said she simply couldn't fall asleep right away.

"*Would* not," I said, after a couple months of this.

"You don't *choose* to fall asleep."

"You choose to try."

"How do you know if I'm trying or not?" She bit into the toast with just her teeth, keeping her lips clean.

"You stay with me for, like, five minutes."

"What good is trying something that won't work? It's a waste of time." She deposited the toast in the trash, brushing her fingers. "Anyhow, what would you know? You're an *easy sleeper*." She made it sound like a personality fault, a lack of refinement.

I was an easy sleeper, though. She was right—or at least I *had* been. As a child, I didn't have nightmares or wet the bed. I didn't wake in a sweat and worry about the shadows raking the windows. I just set my head down and switched off. It didn't feel like I was doing anything at all: it was like digesting food, it was like disappearing. After my father died, my mother let me sleep wherever I wanted because she pitied me, and I frightened her with my resilience. (I did not sob when I heard he'd been in a crash. He did not visit me in my dreams like she told me he would. He did not sit at the foot of my bed and stroke his double chin and say he missed me.) My mother let me sleep in the plastic dog kennel, or under the kitchen table, or sprawled like a beached sea mammal on the living room floor. It suited her to tell her friends I was working through issues of *disorientation*. In truth, I just fell asleep when and where I was tired. I felt I'd been excused from certain human rules that were entirely unrelated to the accident.

By the time I was an adult, I could sleep anywhere I chose. In college, I dozed at the solemn, boring ends of parties and lectures. Later at Fenco, I took tiny, controlled naps at my desk. I propped my chin in my hand, thought about Montana or sea lions, then slipped away and back again. When my colleagues—suspicious, envious—asked, "Were you sleeping, Mason?" it never really seemed that I had. I couldn't understand their resentment. It seemed like an unremarkable function of the body, like pissing or blowing your nose, something that warranted little discussion.

But after A and I got married, after we packed up her brother's car in Winona and moved to Saint Louis, I started thinking about it a lot. In the beginning when A didn't fall asleep after sex, I thought it was just the new place: the way the sheets smelled like a department store and the walls smelled like mold. I thought she was simply nervous, worried that we'd gotten married too quickly and moved too far away from home, to a city neither of us knew. Once, on the Fourth of July, when our neighbors were setting off fireworks on the sidewalk outside our window, she looked at me and said, "You look like someone I've never met." But then she sucked me off, neatly, wiping her chin afterward, and her anxieties seemed natural and temporary. Unfounded. I was sure she felt so, too.

Some nights I'd stay up with her and we'd watch dating shows with couples in hot tubs, people who were drunk and nearly naked and too nervous about the cameras to talk or touch. Sometimes, I felt we were on those dates as well, that we were both sitting there and watching ourselves perform, wondering what the audience would make of us. I said, leaning in, trying to put my arm around her, "That man looks like Jesus. He looks like Jesus, doesn't he? Look at that hair."

She said, "Yes," and for a moment it seemed funny and real. Our marriage.

Still, she wouldn't come to bed—even when the programming switched to infomercials selling dehydrators, close-ups on the screen of wrinkled vegetables like the faces of old men. The host grinned with whitened teeth, and we could not talk about him, he was so painfully enthusiastic. He wanted to sell us dehydrators because he had nothing left to hope for in his career. He had given up, he could not admit it to himself, he had a machine that would shrivel grapes.

I'd eventually wake up with my head in a cushion crack, A gone. I could hear her typing on her laptop in another room.

I thought maybe she was an insomniac. I thought maybe she went through a traumatic event as a child, something she barely knew affected her so deeply. I tried prompting her gently, saying, "A, did you get along with your parents? Did you play well with other kids? Did you have a mean teacher?" I thought I knew how anxieties managed their invisible claws, pulling them in and padding about, like cats. I thought I knew how history surfaced.

And yet, I had to admit A seemed genuinely untroubled. Night after night, long after I'd given up and crawled into bed, I'd wake and find her snoring softly beside me. Her body was small and limp next to mine, so ridiculously peaceful. Beneath my hand, I could feel her breath spread her ribs apart. My own chest felt tight and fixed. I'd lean against her and try to stay awake, try to keep from giving in and forgetting she was there beside me. That's when I began to feel she kept the act of *falling* asleep from me on purpose. It seemed, in a vaguely competitive way, to be a matter of discrimination and attitude. Control.

One morning she wasn't there when I woke up at dawn. I found her crouched on the living room floor with a mixing bowl and long, white gloves. It took me a minute to understand that the gloves were a thin dusting of flour.

"Mason, help me, okay?" She touched her nose with a white knuckle. "You look like I've insulted your hairstyle. What's wrong?"

"What the hell have you been doing?" I didn't say *all night*, I didn't push her.

A sighed. She explained she was folding closed the mouths of dumplings for the Chinese New Year, pinching the white lips around the filling, laying them out in rows. She'd been doing this for hours. Look, the coffee table was covered with them.

She narrowed her eyes. "Did I make too many? Clear off the desk, Mason. We're out of room."

"There are things on the desk."

"That's why I said clear it off. Or I'll do it. Here."

I took the little ball of dough she placed in my hands, but I did not flatten it like she showed me. The dumplings were for the Fengs, who ran an international adoption agency on the first floor of our building. A had invited them to dinner because she had been taken recently with the idea of getting a baby. She'd mentioned it a couple times, but I could never quite follow her reasoning. The idea seemed both too virtuous and too theoretical, a distraction.

"Have you been writing someone online? Is this an internet thing?"

A shook her head and looked sorry, as if I'd made a mistake too predictable to correct. "Yes, Mason, if that's what you want to think. Yes. I have a virtual lover and I fuck him in my thoughts."

We boiled the dumplings and watched them bloat, surge to the surface. Then we lifted them out one by one with a slotted spoon, separating the mangled ones from the clean ones. We were surprisingly good at work like this, jobs that required careful sorting and not much communication. The morning sun lit up the pale, downy hair beneath A's left ear. We agreed to eat the worst dumplings right away, stabbing them with forks and waving away steam. The good ones, yellow, stuffed as satchels, we wrapped in foil and froze for the Fengs.

Our marriage had always depended, to a certain extent, on recognizing together the difference between public and private consumption.

I brought home gifts. I bought a black eye mask with satin ribbons that tied in the back, the sort of thing rich widows wear in movies. I purchased medicinal herbs, a new comforter, earplugs that looked like green gumdrops. I got a small fan that clipped onto the back of the bed and hummed gently, erasing other sounds with white noise. At first, A was surprised by my efforts, then amused. At the dinner table, she put on the mask and earplugs, groping her way around to my side and knocking the salt in a white spray on the floor. She sang, "Marco! Marco! Marco!"

I told her I was trying to make things easier for her.

"What?"

I took her in my lap and plucked out her earplugs. When she pulled off the mask, her hair got caught in the ribbons and she had to fiddle with the knot.

I repeated what I said, and she sighed. "Mason, what is this *really* about?"

I got angry then because she didn't know, and it seemed simple enough. She seemed rested and oblivious, energetic even. She wasn't irritable in the way of people who have been deprived of sleep. Her eyes were not red and weepy. Rather she was vital and pitying, looking down at me and stroking my hair. She seemed unnatural to me, unnecessarily cold. I stood up, scooting her off my lap, freeing myself from the bright health of her body. "I'm not the one here who's messed up," I informed her. "Don't make it seem like that."

My alarm went off when it was still dark, and I waited for the rush of bitterness to wake me up, the discovery of A's absence. By now my injustice felt familiar and correct, a superior moral position. It was almost disappointing to find A there, curled around me innocently as sheets. I nudged her awake. "Get up. Have breakfast," but she didn't even open her eyes. She said she was sleeping. She said, "Good night."

I left her like that, coiled under blankets, and arrived at work earlier than usual. It was a hole of an office, but I appreciated the way it stayed the same day after day. It was always chilly and brightly lit. I thought I was performing my job decently enough, but one day Mabel from Financing surprised me by touching my hand when we were eating lunch. She said, "Tell me what's wrong with you, Mason."

I stared at her. "You have mayonnaise on your thumb."

She licked it off. "You don't seem happy."

I didn't like that I liked her sympathy. Three years ago, Mabel suffered a stroke so now her right eye drooped sorrowfully. She had a way of tilting her head that made her appear very focused and very young, the way a precocious, unloved child might look at you.

"My wife won't sleep with me," I confessed.

"Is she sleeping with someone else? Do you know who she's with?" Mabel's look was the same as it always was: appalled and interested.

I admitted I did not.

She took a minute to think this over. Then she grew matter-of-fact, pulling a hard-boiled egg from her sack and prying off bits of shell with a fingernail. She told me there were certain ways to deal with these things. Did I know what she meant, she asked. I shook my head. She told me I needed to go fuck the guy up, whoever he was.

"Won't that just make the situation worse?" But my heart was pounding.

"Mason, this is for *you*. Not the *situation*."

That night, I spent a few hours after work at McDuffy's downtown, and when I got home it was late, bright-gloomy, the sky lighter than you'd expect for ten thirty, like an empty stadium before the last light goes out. I found A on a stepladder in our living room, wearing a pastel cooking apron and reading glasses. She'd pushed the furniture to the center of the room and purchased a tall column of paint canisters: bright white to cover the dull white that was there before. She asked if I wanted to help out, but I didn't like how the new paint was so shiny under A's brush, how it went on like saliva in long, wet streaks. I could only tell that it was there for a few seconds before it started to dry, disappear.

"Come to bed?" I asked her.

I hadn't yet set down my bag, my umbrella.

She murmured, "Not yet, not yet."

I looked at her then, at her thin, bony face, and remembered how she once smoothed down her eyebrows with lip balm. We'd been at my mother's house, between courses, and she'd seemed so ingenious and strange to me then, almost horrible.

I didn't want to beg.

"Can't the rest wait?" My throat ached. I wanted to touch her and get away, all at once.

"It can't."

I thought of the dumplings, now icy rocks in the freezer. "Is this to impress the Fengs, too?"

"It's for us," she corrected carefully. "*We* live here."

I do not stay up with A anymore; I do not indulge her. I leave the door open when I go to bed so I can hear her moving around out there, the shift of the floorboards when she steps, the water running in the sink. I tell myself I'm not waiting for her, but my mind, when I start awake and scan the room, feels scraped open, empty. At two, the lights from the next-door gas station turn off and the room swings into a deeper darkness. This seems to make things clearer to me for an instant. I sit up and lie back down. I try to retrieve some thought that has scrabbled its tiny claws over me. I can hear A in the other room humming "Grand Ole Flag." I can hear her lover in there, too: I want him to be there, I dream him, I make him up. I hate him so much it makes me sick, but that's not a bad feeling at all. It's a decent, natural sort of loathing. He is, after all, rugged and self-involved, the sort of guy I snubbed in college. Probably A has put him to work, and he's good at it too: dipping his brush deep into the can, running it up and down in easy, gliding lines. While he's working, A sets about exploring him in her practical way, like a landscape or the face of some pretty cliff. She believes she's keeping him quiet, touching him slowly with her fingers from behind, setting one hand over his dick and one hand over his mouth. But the reason he's quiet is because he has nothing to say. He keeps her busy. He doesn't want or need anything. He fucks her on the floor and leaves before she's through.

A has turned off all the lights. I can hear her in the bathroom, and then she's out. She's standing in the doorway. I think I see her standing in the doorway, but I can't tell. I want to flick on the lights and catch her walking in, catch the startled look on her face, the wince. But she does not come.

Then I think: with those hands that painted our walls, A's lover will surprise her. He's unpredictable, powerful. He won't stand in some lake and wait like I did—his nipples turning into scabs—while A hides beneath the surface. He will not shiver and despise her. I think A's lover will dive under, open his eyes, see A's scrawny white legs and drifting white arms, grab her. And she will shriek. She'll scare the ducks bobbing on the surface of the lake. He'll pull her hair with his hand.

As always when I wake up near dawn, A is sleeping gently.

On the day the Fengs were coming to dinner, A asked me to be home early. She called me at work in the afternoon, anxiously describing a cucumber she wanted, and I could feel each coil on the phone cord, each plasticky noose around my finger. I was exhausted, inarticulate, but I could still say what I needed to say. I told her I'd come.

I put on my jacket and shut down the computer, deciding to take a little nap in the car before I drove home. In truth, I could feel the nap before it started, that ready nest of darkness like a hole I'd dug, a secret burrow. Mabel walked out to the parking lot with me because she wanted a ride to her bus stop. She held my wrist, and her hand was thick and wet, immovable. I told her I was going to take a nap before I went anywhere, just for five minutes. She said, fine, she'd wait.

I cranked back the driver's seat and opened the window, watching a bit of snow catch in the gray air and drop. For a second I leaned back and everything stopped. But then I felt a throb in my hips and neck, my gut clenching. The snow swirled and covered the windshield and blew off, miraculously disappearing. I didn't feel sleepy at all. I felt as though I were riding my body to someplace new, somewhere more interesting.

"Awake already?" Mabel asked from the passenger seat.

"I can't sleep," I confessed. It seemed that I'd discovered something A had kept from me. "I can't sleep, but I'm so tired!" I was exhilarated by the prospect.

Mabel groaned, shaking her vulture face. She turned on the radio and commanded me to close my eyes as NPR warned of hurricanes abroad, then bled into tinny banjos and an old man crooning.

"For Pete's sake," Mabel said, impatiently soothing. "You got to relax."

I told her it wouldn't work. I explained that it wasn't as easy as that. But then my eyes were closed, and it was.

When the Fengs arrived for dinner, they took off their shoes at the door and tiptoed around in black socks with gold toes. They hadn't been to our apartment before, and they wanted to see if it was the same layout as their office on the first floor. Polite and appreciative, they liked best the objects we hung on our walls. "Nice clock," they said. "Good calendar."

I admit this praise made me vaguely proud, as if our belongings revealed some measure of discernment I hadn't known we possessed. I could tell A was pleased as well. She kept touching items on tables, straightening pillows, running her hands over glasses and chairs. She said, bashfully, "We painted in here, but it doesn't look very different."

"Very white!" Mrs. Feng pointed out, so A blushed with pleasure.

When the Lenten bells started ringing down the street, we negotiated places at the dinner table and hovered over our chairs until Mrs. Feng sat down. She laughed because the table came up to her chest. She looked like our gray, obedient child, poised for a test of etiquette at her first dinner party. Mr. Feng came with a pillow from the couch, and she stood up gracefully and sat down again, a choreographed set of movements. Someone's strand of hair drifted over the candles.

A and I brought out the dumplings and sauces. We had boiled the dumplings a second time and piled their slippery bodies in the center of a large platter. They shined like yellow shells washed up on a shore, but when we bit into them they were rubbery and difficult to swallow.

"Happy New Year!" A cried, embarrassed.

"Happy to you!" Mrs. Feng said. And Mr. Feng nodded, apparently approving.

When did A and I relax? I thought about how eager we must look to the Fengs, how young and happy. The Fengs had been in the United States for twenty years, but it seemed important to impress them with our American vitality. I wanted them to be envious.

After a while, Mr. Feng asked A, "Where do you work?" and A said, "I've taken some time off since we moved. To get, you know, settled." She looked over at me and shrugged. "We were hoping to start a family, but things haven't worked out just right yet."

By then Mr. Feng was pushing a dumpling into his mouth, but Mrs. Feng set her chopsticks down and looked at A in a way I didn't quite understand, almost tenderly. She began describing her own children in a serious and well-organized fashion, as if arguing the merits of politicians she wanted us to support. She called them her babies, though they were now in their thirties and ran a software development company. Her babies spoke German and collected orchids, apparently, as well as other exotic flowers whose names I did not recognize and could not bring myself to imagine. When A started asking questions, I went to the kitchen and arranged the fruit on a plate. Tiny oranges, green apples, grapes. I peeled the oranges and plucked out the luminous, half-moon shapes, a bright citrus scent filling the room.

I announced, "I heard fruit on the Lunar New Year brings good luck!"

Mr. Feng turned to me. "Yes, and new clothes." He scooted his chair out and lifted a black-socked foot, wiggling his gold toes gamely. By that time, he'd had more than a bit of wine.

I nodded, almost delighted, almost careless now. "What else?"

"Money!" Mrs. Feng laughed.

"I always want good dreams," Mr. Feng said. "Did you dream last night?"

I had. The dream came back to me then, extraordinary and clear, like a flush of good fortune. It seemed I had never dreamt so vividly before, and I wanted everyone to know that I, too, was blessed by portents. I wanted A to know this, to see how well I could get along. "It was about my dead father!"

Mr. Feng clapped his hands. "Good boy! What did father say?"

It seemed important to remember exactly. I had never dreamt of him before, could barely even conjure him in my memory. But now I could see him wobbling his double chins in my dream, moving something in his hands, mumbling. The image made me think of a priest with a rosary, or an old-fashioned merchant with an abacus. A man distracted. "He was counting, maybe?"

"How much, how much?" Mrs. Feng sounded truly interested.

I started to make something up, to keep them clapping and pleased, but then I glanced at A and hesitated. Her face was very still and white.

I touched her hand attentively. "Sweetie, you okay?"

"Can I get anyone anything else?" she asked. She stood up then, reaching past me for the platter of gray dumplings. I thought perhaps she didn't feel very well suddenly, but as she leaned over the table, she hissed in my ear, "You said *gone*."

"I said what?" I looked at the Fengs.

She straightened up, breathing in sharply. When she spoke again, her voice had jumped a hissy octave. "That's what you always said, like he'd left." Her lips pulled up strangely over her front teeth. "You never once said *dead*."

"I *did*," I promised the Fengs. "My dad," I explained, gratuitously.

But then it seemed I'd used the wrong tone or word, and I tried to correct myself. "My father," I tried, apologetically. "When I was a kid—"

But A was already on her way to the kitchen. "Excuse me," I said to the Fengs, who were silent now, looking down at their chopsticks. Gently, I patted the napkin on my plate, pausing a moment to watch the soy sauce bleed into the wadded paper. Then I stood up.

In the kitchen, A was scraping the last of the dumplings into the trash with a fork.

"Hon?" I asked her. I felt wary and, under that, just a prick of irritation.

She shook her head without looking up.

"Hey—" I said, reaching out with my hand.

She took a step back. "Christ, Mason." She was speaking to the dumplings as she slid them into the trash. "Who does that? Who doesn't say that?" Her eyes were shiny as scales when she looked up at me. "What kind of person doesn't ever say *dead*?"

I used to think the danger of marriage was getting too close, losing track of the differences between you and the other. The spring after we were married, for instance, A and I took a trip to Itasca, the place where the Mississippi started in a lake still white with ice. A took her shoes off and picked her way across the creek's mouth: cringing, almost singing with the pain of the barely unfrozen water. It took longer to cross than she expected it would, and when I went over the bridge and met her on the other side, her eyes were watering. I sat her down on a picnic table and put her icy feet in the baggy pockets of my coat, one on each side, her legs open in front of me. I said, softly patting the bulges in my pockets, "Hey, look what I found in the Mississippi!" She giggled noisily, closed her eyes.

I say this because there were times when I felt useful to her, worthy. I remember thinking we'd avoided the pitfalls other couples had fallen into, the gooey, nonchalant forms of intimacy. Every point of connection for us, even after two years of marriage, seemed precious to me, continually rare. I say this because I was honestly surprised when I looked at the pictures from that trip and there was not a single one of us together. There's me standing in the shadow of Paul Bunyan's statue, A frowning forlornly at a diagram of ants. I know the explanation is simple—with two people, there's just the one taking the picture and the one posing out in front— and yet it never occurred to me until I saw the pictures at home just how painful this made things when you looked back on them.

After the Fengs left, I expected to lie awake for a long time, but I fell asleep right away, effortlessly, without even crawling under the covers. I tipped in and out of dreams. I couldn't remember anything particular when I woke. I just had the feeling that I'd been dreaming and I should go back: there was so much work to be done, there was all that complicated maneuvering.

Once, I woke and went to the window. I realized I was looking out there for the room I'd just come from, the one from my dream.

Once, I woke with A in my arms, like I'd scavenged her body from a riot. I said, "Where did you come from?"

She murmured, "I've been here all along."

I said, "You're lying."

She sounded sad. "You're the liar, Mason. You must know that."

Late in the week, Mrs. Feng left a message on our answering machine about coming downstairs to their office. A didn't mention the message to me, and neither of us erased it. It stayed a blinking red light on the phone, distracting but innocuous.

At work, Mabel stopped me outside the men's room. She took my elbow and asked what I did to the guy with my wife. She had two white bits of saliva in the corners of her mouth, wiggling like maggots when she talked, making me nervous. I was suddenly disgusted by her lopsided face. "Why would you accuse someone you don't even know?" I demanded. When I walked away, I noticed I was trembling.

It seems I'm left watching A watching me during dinner. She looks like she's waiting to say something. "Everything alright?" I ask. Our plates are strewn with the needle bones of fish.

She takes my hand, walks me to the unmade bed, lies down. Then she fucks me, very swiftly, very proficiently, holding my hips in her hands like handles. I feel shaken up afterward. A works her toes into her socks, clips closed her bra and stands up.

I feel a panic rising in me. "Don't go?" Her hair is in her face.

She makes a ponytail, pulling an elastic band from her wrist in a sleight-of-hand maneuver, a sudden flick of her fingers. "I'm not tired yet."

"Then just lie down and wait."

"Mason, you can't make me stay." Her tone is even, controlled.

"Just try to sleep."

"I *can't*. I cannot *make* myself." Now her eyes are red. I can see them very well. The tightness of her ponytail seems to have made them wider.

I tug her back to the bed. "Just stay for ten seconds," I say, as she moves her lips away from mine. She starts to stand up, so I lean on her, grab her wrists, push her back.

"Stop it, Mason," she says.

I hold her down. She has a new expression in her eyes, one that makes me feel heavier than I did, my limbs oddly sluggish. She tries to push me off, but I still have her fists in my hands, those tiny rocks, those little knuckles and fingers. She makes a sound then, a squeak, which I cover up with one hand. For just a second, I cover her whole face with my palm and fingers. I can feel her legs start to kick behind me. I can feel her sinking—into the mattress, into the pillows and sheets—but her face gets slippery and my hand slides off. I take hold of her hair.

What she's doing, I notice, is crying with her eyes closed.

"A—" I whisper.

"Fucking bastard!" she says.

It occurs to me later, after A's left with a backpack of clothes, that the baby A wants might already be born. I consider that he's somewhere across the world even as I lie in bed, learning to hold his head up and suck watery formula from a bottle. The thought makes me feel morose, nostalgic. I feel as though I've missed something important, something I should have known about and prepared for long ago. I wonder, what if he's four or five already? What if he can read and write? What if he's already old enough to resent my absence in his life, the gaping space between him and his future? I think about him—a ten-year-old in China with a shoebox of drawings, sketches of American wildlife he's seen on postcards—and regret wastes in my limbs. When A comes back, I think, we'll have to call the Fengs and explain to them that we need to hurry.

I get up and decide to make the bed, that neat square, but once it's made, I can't resist crawling back under the blankets. A's side of the bed feels like another part of the world. I set her earplugs in my ears and pull on her mask. I lie back in the darkness to wait for her, but there sleep is instead: faceless, pitiless, and perfect.

GIMME SHELTER

In her adulthood strangers asked, "Where'd you get your accent?" They guessed England, they guessed Sweden, they guessed the South. She'd shrug, even as an adult. It pleased her to have her words come out of her mouth with no fixed address, as if the English she spoke was soft and malleable.

*

In that house where she grew up there were seven rooms, but once she dreamed of an eighth. Behind the washing machine and dusty finches' cage, she found a secret door that opened to a nineteenth-century library. There were bookcases covering the walls, a red oriental carpet, a long rectangular window at the ceiling. In her dream she felt a sweet despair: what beautiful things her parents kept from her! She understood then that they were just a little cruel, to hide the best room in the house from their children.

*

Their bedroom was on the second floor. Dark, walled in pine boards with knots like faces. As a child, Lynn used to nap in their bed and feel watched. She didn't like going to sleep when it was light and waking up in the dark. She felt that something of hers had been stolen. Beneath the floor she heard their voices—the voices of people who'd had afternoons. She hated them because they left her alone with her sleep, which was like a soft animal that crawled onto her chest and slowly suffocated her.

*

Her sister said they should carry their dolls outside and set them on the driveway for someone to find, someone better. The dolls had faces that had been chewed on by dogs. "Look at them," Henna said, grim and self-righteous. But they weren't ruined! The dogs had left them slippery with drool, but they still had all their parts. When you pressed the button on her arm, Isabella still opened her mouth and cried.

Still, the tiny pockmarks were like a disease of the skin she could neither cure nor imagine away.

Henna lined them up on the asphalt, tiny arms open and waiting. The sign under the mailbox said SAVE US.

Lynn stayed in the house and watched through a crack in the curtains. The babies looked like garbage. They looked like war. A boy came by on his bike, eyed them, and asked, "Do you have any baseball cards?"

Henna said, "No." She was drawing hearts on her shoe with a pen.

The boy said, "Do you have anything good?"

*

Her parents' room was at the top of a narrow staircase, the only room on the second floor. It had steeply sloped ceilings, a worn gray carpet, a door that locked. When Henna turned thirteen, her parents moved out, dragged their dismantled bedframe to the unfinished basement. Henna set her collection of glass cats on their windowsill. She covered the pine-knot faces in the wall with her posters of Nadia Comaneci.

In the other bedroom, the one on the first floor of the house, Lynn's brother moved out of his crib and into the bunk below her. He did not sleep soundly, as Henna had, but turned and turned under his dreams. It was like bobbing in a rickety boat, the way the wooden bunk bed creaked and shifted beneath her. Lynn said, "Saul, Saul?" hanging her head down to peek at him. The mice turned their wheels in their glass cage.

*

This is the story her father told her: the house was given in debt or payment to her grandfather's father. It belonged first to a farmer, though no one knew what kind, and they set it on wheels and drove it with flashing lights to the new edge of the city. As a child, Lynn thought often of the farmer who gave it up, who stood in a field somewhere and watched it go like a parade.

They dug a foundation from the hillside and set it down by the pond. The house was clapboard and square, brown-shuttered. In the beginning, it was like a body without limbs, just the most important rooms, the ones you need to stay alive. Then her young grandfather added the upstairs bedroom and garage, covered the back bathroom in pale blue tiles, screened in the open porch. He used the parts of other houses no one wanted anymore. Her grandfather had worked in demolition before auto repair in the years after the war, and he'd pilfered other people's old doors, their cracked windowpanes and tiles, their long, skittery moldings.

*

When the mice got loose, they lived for a while in the heating ducts. You could hear them running past, their claws ticking in the metal pipes, their bodies shushing against the walls. Then they settled under the refrigerator and made babies. Lynn set her ear on the linoleum and shined a flashlight into the narrow crack. They blinked their black, identical eyes. Their babies looked like pale pink stools.

She didn't know how the mice got out of their cage, but she didn't tell her parents. When her mother put Saul to bed—a purse on her shoulder, a sock in her hand—Lynn made a show of filling the blue plastic bowl with seed. She declared, "Midget and Dill look sleepy!" burrowing her finger in some wood shavings.

After her mother left for her night shift at the hospital, Lynn lifted the bowl of food from the cage and emptied it in the toilet. The black seeds floated on the green surface. She flushed and flushed.

"Poopy, poopy, poopy!" Saul said when she got back.

She hissed at him, "*Baby!*"

*

During the summer, her parents carried the TV out to the porch where it was cooler. There were no curtains or shades, just a crimped rusty screen from knee to ceiling. You could hear the TV from down the street, and at night a blue glow lit up the front yard.

Sometimes Lynn stopped her bike outside at dusk and listened. There was the sound of the cottonwoods against the roof, like a flock of nervous birds, and the dogs at the back door whining. There was a gunshot on television. There was the sound of her mother on the porch, saying, "Just a carpet for the hallway. Just a machine with a button you can push."

Her father said, "Just a dishwasher is more complicated than that."

The TV said, "The polar bear is nearly extinct."

*

After her parents moved to the basement, her mother started making plans for the house. She wanted to add a new wing to the back, with a sliding glass door that opened onto a deck. She wanted a sink that didn't leak into a bucket. She got a beautiful, determined look on her face and walked from room to room, squinting at walls. She made the bathroom into a closet; she made the bedroom into a two-car garage. She asked Henna, "Would you like wallpaper for your new room? Do you want carpet or wood?"

Henna was suspicious. She worried that her room would no longer be the nicest in the house. She said, mimicking their father, "What an asinine suggestion! There's no money for that."

Lynn saw her mother blink and pull a lock of wet hair from Henna's mouth. She used two pinched fingers, as if extracting something from a puddle. "Yuck, Henna," she said. "Yuck."

At dinner, Henna sat next to their father, who had flecks of grease on his hands from his auto body shop. He hit the ketchup bottle with one swift blow against his palm. "Pass the sauerkraut," he said.

Their mother kept it. She described the new kitchen she wanted: the wall she wanted to knock down, the new white linoleum. She made it sound like a country she planned to visit, somewhere far away and scenic, a place they might all go to together. The Kitchen.

Their father pulled some leaky ketchup from the bottle with a knife. "Don't be asinine, Linda."

She looked at him.

He said, "Well, really."

Their mother was quiet. She had a mechanical anger, Lynn knew, like a wind-up gear. She needed a second to turn the screw and let it release. Then their mother tipped a bowl over and emptied all the sauerkraut onto her plate. It covered everything—her peas, her hotdog, her tiny wad of gum. It slid onto the table.

"That wasn't necessary," their father said.

Their mother said, "Of *course* not."

*

Lynn described the library dream once to her lover. She remembered everything: the shiny wooden shelves, the walls of weathered books, the dense smell of old carpet. It was so clear it seemed possible to go back, to fill the car with gas and drive through the night, to find the key under the birdbath by the door, climb down the damp stairs, and open the tiny, hidden door behind the hanging laundry. She knew how the doorknob would feel (a little sticky, cool) and the ten even steps from one side of the room to the other. At the same time, she knew it was impossible to go to the library just like it was impossible to return to that house, which had been so neatly crushed by a single cottonwood. The trunk of the tree came down through the roof one night, splintering rafters and shingles and walls, then lay quietly in the upstairs room like a new piece of furniture.

*

When their father bought the new couch at Sears, he wrapped it in tarps and drove it home in the bed of his pick-up. Bound in clear plastic, it looked like the giant larva of a huge insect, something waiting to hatch. Their mother stood in the driveway, saying, "What is that? What is that?" her hands on her hips.

Their father smiled and blushed. He sliced through the twine with a utility knife and slit open the plastic. The pale upholstery was the color of skin after a burn, perfect and impossibly pink. He helped their mother into the bed of the truck, and she looked like a prom queen up there, waving shyly at them all, perched primly on her new pink couch. Lynn could tell she didn't want to look too pleased. "It won't match, Alec," she complained. "It's too *much*." Then she leaned back and shrieked, "It's like being swallowed!"

*

Their neighbors, the Kenyons, had twin girls who played the violin. On the street, you could hear them practicing—tight little scales, lively arpeggios like stones skipped in water. They also had a Siamese cat they dressed in doll clothes, who wandered in calico on their roof. The Kenyon girls were several years younger than Lynn, but sometimes they saw her in a tree somewhere and climbed up after. They were polite and affectionate. They slapped mosquitoes on Lynn's bare legs. From time to time, they kissed each other on the lips and wanted to kiss Lynn too, but Lynn climbed out of reach.

When Mrs. Kenyon came out of the house, Lynn knew there'd be trouble. Mrs. Kenyon yelled, "Alia! Megan!" pulling hoses around on the grass, pointing sprinklers at beds of hostas. Lynn scrambled up as high as she could get, but the Kenyon girls cried, "Mom! Mom!" dangling precariously. They wanted Mrs. Kenyon to be afraid for them, which she was. She ran to the broad trunk of the tree and put her hands in the air, as if planning to catch them. She yelped, "Careful!" grabbing at their ankles, which made it difficult for the girls to climb down.

On the ground, they giggled and sobbed. "We're alright! We're alright!" they said, as if surprised by this outcome.

Mrs. Kenyon glared up into the branches. "Lynn!"

Lynn slid slowly down, barely moving her body.

Mrs. Kenyon put her hands on her hips. "Lynn, you're the older one, take some responsibility." She turned to the girls. "For the rest of the day, you can play *inside*."

The Kenyon girls—red-eyed with tears, with excitement—said, "Can we go to Lynn's house, then?"

Mrs. Kenyon and Lynn said, "No!"

But Lynn didn't like how Mrs. Kenyon walked the girls back across the street, one in each hand, like luggage.

She revised to *maybe*, calling after them across the street: "Maybe tomorrow! Maybe the day after that!"

*

Each night that summer, Lynn filled the plastic bowl in the empty glass cage. She spun the metal wheel with her hand and ruffled the shavings. In the kitchen, she aimed a flashlight under the refrigerator and watched the mice clean their whiskers with their twiggy hands. The babies fumbled for their parents' flanks, doddering and unsteady on their feet, holding their tails stiff for balance.

Once when she clicked the light into the humming darkness, they were gone.

She put her face against the sticky linoleum, her cheek, her ear. The mice were gone, but not their babies. They were white and dry as bits of powdered donuts, except for the red on the places where they were chewed in half.

She clicked the light off and on again. Off and on.

In her room, Lynn filled the food in the cage, checked the water, and smoothed down the shavings. She touched an old pellet of poop, hard as the tiniest of glass beads. She said to Saul, who was watching her from his bed, "Do you want to play with the mice, Sauly?"

He sat up, excited, shoving the covers off. "Yes!"

She made a cup with her hands and crawled into bed with him. "Careful," she warned. "You have to be very, very careful with tiny animals."

He held out his hands, rigid with pleasure, waiting for Dill to walk in.

*

The morning their mother didn't come home from her night shift and their father left early for work, they stayed in bed. At first they lay beneath the covers, thrilled by their unexpected fortune. When the sun grew hot on the blankets, they got up for snacks, for buttered sugar on bread, then climbed back under the sheets and waited. They waited for someone to come by—the bus driver, the neighbors—and worry on their behalf. It felt like a holiday or disaster to be in bed like this, a very special occasion.

But no one came, and Henna grew lonely in her upstairs room, so she coaxed Lynn and Saul out to the porch. The TV was there, leftover from the humid summer days, so they sat in frayed wicker chairs and watched cartoons. The day was bright and hot, though it was already September. The kindergartners were riding home on buses. In another part of the city, Lynn's class was learning cursive and drawing Mars in glossy books. In another house down the street, someone was cleaning the welcome mat with a vacuum.

The postman with his blue satchel came up the driveway. He waved at them cheerfully through the screen. "Hey, there!" he called, but then his expression grew puzzled. "You kids off from school?"

Henna shot up from her chair, nodding, then shaking her head. "Well, actually, we're sick today!" She opened the door a tiny crack to cough and take the mail. Her face was bright red.

After the postman left, Henna turned off the TV and rushed them inside. Lynn could see certain realities were beginning to dawn on her. "This is my first *tardy!*" she said. "My first one all year!"

She looked at Lynn and Saul like it was all their idea.

They went back to bed. Saul didn't want to, but Henna held him down and explained, "We're sick today!" She was worried now about what her new middle school teachers would say. She wanted an excused absence.

Lynn coaxed him. "Bang, bang," she said, and Saul lay back on the pillows because he liked games where he got shot. Henna decided to sleep in Lynn's bed, where she curled up in a ball and coughed. "Stop it," Lynn whispered, but Henna countered, "I'm *sick* today, Lynn!"

Lynn's sleep was white and despairing. She kept thinking she was crawling out of bed, putting on her shoes, going outside, but then she'd wake and find her head heavy on the pillow. Henna was chewing a lock of her own hair, pulling it from her mouth and making a dark spoke that pointed straight at the ceiling. Beneath them, Saul was either gone or so still he was hardly breathing. Lynn closed her eyes and let sleep drop its soft animal body—crushing her, turning her over—then she opened her eyes again. That's when she saw their mother in the doorway.

Their mother was staring at them, confused.

"What's this?" She rushed in and lifted Saul in her arms, shaking him. "Did your father leave you like this?" Her fly was open. Her shoes were off.

She grabbed Lynn's ankle and almost pulled her from bed. She kneeled on the floor and rifled through dirty clothes, lifting and discarding garments. "What were you thinking?" she accused them.

She turned on Henna last and said, "You're not even *dressed!*"

Henna backed into the corner of Lynn's bed, her eyes red, her knees pulled up inside of her T-shirt.

"We're sick," Lynn pleaded. She wanted her mother to feel how hot she was; she wanted to reach for her hand and put it on her head. She got up on her knees and begged her mother, "We're in bed because we're *sick*."

*

Every fall, her father opened a door in the ceiling of Henna's room and disappeared into the attic. He set traps for the wild animals that wintered there—the squirrels, the raccoons, the mice. The traps were simple coils of wire, and they looked like something friendly you should talk into, primitive phones, the doorbells you can build from kits.

The fall after the mice escaped, Lynn asked to follow him up the ladder to lay the traps. She'd read books about attics and imagined giant rafters, shuttered windows, furniture draped in white sheets. She wanted to see the sort of room that was on top of everything. But this attic felt like a hole in the ground. Her father said, "Don't stand up. Scoot on your butt. Distribute your weight evenly."

When her father clicked on the flashlight, she saw that the roof was just inches from their heads, pink insulation sagging. Lynn reached up and unwound her hair from a nail.

"This house was built in 1901 by a *pioneer.*"

Lynn sneezed. "I know that." She'd heard the story and wanted something else, some other tunnel to the past, another line of history. The tiny attic made her dizzy.

Her father handed Lynn the flashlight to hold as he pried open the wire mouth of a trap. Then he set down a Girl Scout cookie, frozen since spring, when Lynn had knocked on other people's doors and stood in their warm hallways.

The cookie glinted white with frost.

He said, "This will take those little buggers out." But he seemed sorry about it, as if it were an unpleasant requirement of fatherhood, the ritual kill. He secured the cookie on the platform.

Lynn asked, "Where does it get them?"

He hesitated. "By their necks." And she could tell by his voice he was pleased with her question, pleased to see she understood that being alive in the world meant a series of such indignities, of killing and being killed.

He scooted backward into her. "You want to come with me to pick up the animals?"

Lynn thought of the black, blinking eyes of the mice, the split-open slugs of their babies. She didn't want to come back for them. She said, "Yes."

*

Their father and Saul were home when the tree came down, waiting out the storm in the basement. Everyone else was away that night: their mother working at the hospital, Henna at college, Lynn in a car with a boy she loved painfully, who sang long, fretting songs for her and recorded them on cassette tapes. Lynn watched the storm from a hilltop across town, the boy's off-key voice coming through the speakers, the boy's hand on her leg. She loved this boy but was a little bored. She'd heard this song before. The boy's cassette voice sang, "War, children, it's just a shot a way. Juuust a shot away."

Saul said the tree shook the whole house. It made the washing machine shudder next to them in the basement and knocked the finches' cage down to the floor. The birds swooped out the open cage door and up the stairway. Their father followed, and then Saul, with the cordless phone clenched in his hand, tapping out 9-1-1, though of course the line was dead.

The dogs stayed trembling in the basement.

Upstairs, wet plaster from the kitchen ceiling lay in a scattered dark mound on the linoleum. Up one more flight of stairs, in Henna's room, it was raining. First they saw a few wet, green branches heaped against the dresser, and then the long, white trunk, nestled deeply in the collapsed rafters. Saul said later it looked like an endangered animal, something you're not supposed to be able to see in your lifetime, huge and very, very tired.

Saul was a bookish teenager, the sort with very few friends.

*

One year, the Kenyons asked Lynn to cat-sit for them when they went to Disney World. They showed her how to empty the kitty litter and carry the cat's bowl to the kitchen, where the water was cleaned by a special filter in the tap. They gave her the code for the garage, and she walked over there before her brother and sister woke up, letting the garage door rumble closed behind her. She was very good at this job, responsible and conscientious. She did things she wasn't asked: she watered the violets and emptied the wastepaper basket. She watched movies in their basement—black-and-white classics with nervous ladies—the cat stepping daintily over her stretched-out legs. She ate chewy Cheetos from their cabinets. She lay down on the girls' beds, which were in separate but identical yellow rooms, and enjoyed their separate but identical pillows. She took a shower. She used their soap and towels. She put on the girls' socks, too small for her, but clean and tight as slippers. She went into their parents' room and read the notes in their coat pockets: *Home at 6. Meet you at King Tut. Get Milk.*

*

When her mother stooped next to the cage and asked, "Where are the mice?" Lynn was calm, almost surprised that she'd asked. By then the mice had been gone for several weeks, the babies born, killed, and rotted, their stench ripe for a few days but long since faded.

She said, "What do you mean, where?"

Her mother tapped the empty cage with a painted nail. "I mean, where are they?"

Lynn was on her bed, smoothing the fur of a bear flat then rough. "They must be there," she said.

"They're not." Her mother pried the lid open. Inside, the shavings were crisp and blond as the dyed hair of old ladies.

Lynn asked, "Did they get out?" touching the bear's blue plastic eye.

"Oh, no." Her mother straightened up and looked around at the floor. She nudged a pair of jeans with her toe.

Lynn said, trying to sound worried and sad, "Do you think Saul tried to hold them?"

"Oh, *no*."

"Oh, no," Lynn said.

*

She called her parents one night when she was living in a city with mountains and a cereal factory. That was when she could smell burnt popcorn all day, a cheap movie-theater scent in every room and park and office. She called her parents late at night, balancing her address book on her lap because she had never memorized the number for their new apartment. The phone rang and rang. They'd lived in that apartment for more than a decade. The ringing seemed to go on and on, and she thought, *It's happened, they're gone*, and once she thought it, she wished it true, her grief over it was so good, so complete, so utterly wasting. There was no other way to feel about them in the world. There was grief or nothing.

Of course her mother answered the phone, breathless, and said, "God, Lynn, you must be desperate!" Then she wasn't anymore.

*

She had dreams about the fallen cottonwood, and dreams about the library under the house, and sometimes dreams about her mother. In the dreams, her mother had hands that curled up slightly and a button on her chest that you could press to make her talk. She said "Save Me," but Lynn would not.

One year her mother asked her to go for a walk after Thanksgiving dinner. There were still a few hours before Lynn's plane left the city, so they bundled up and set out. By then, her mother was a little stooped, shaky from a recent hip operation. They walked slowly past the apartment complexes and condos, past the new subdivisions with their shoveled sidewalks, past the old highway to the quarry on the other side of town. There, sumac rattled brittle leaves. The wind swept up the snow in shrouds.

"It's pretty here," Lynn said, feeling an unfamiliar lightness. She remembered riding her bike through these quarry dunes as a child. She remembered falling off and carrying a gravelly wound home on her arm. For a second, she felt a sentimental protectiveness—for the injured girl pushing her bike, for her mother, hobbling enthusiastically through the snow, for the past, which was so pitiful and distant.

"Look out," Lynn warned. Her mother was climbing up a drift of snow, and Lynn took her mittened hand in her own, steadying her.

She said, almost tenderly, "Mom, Mom." The sun had slid behind the dunes. "Should we go back?"

"You were always the worrier, Lynn."

"It's just, it's getting late."

"You were always my favorite, though."

Lynn turned. This was something their mother said to all of them at one time or another. Still, it worked like a blow to the chest. In the last light, Lynn could just make out her mother's face: her bright red nose, her slightly parted lips. For a second, she despised the needy way her mother smiled, the way her beanie was slipping to the very top of her head and would soon fall off. She wanted something from Lynn, of course, but Lynn walked on, carefully saying nothing.

They continued to the edge of the old highway, which was difficult to distinguish because it hadn't been plowed. A few ragged tire-lines marked it.

"I have an idea." Lynn felt her mother's mitten on her arm, the heavy weight of that woolen paw. "Let's go by the old house on the way back."

Lynn grew impatient. "No, Mom."

"Why shouldn't we?"

"You hated that place."

"That's where you grew up!" Her mother sounded offended.

"You called it a *dump*."

Her mother winced. "Don't you even want to see what happened to it?"

She did not. In Lynn's mind, it had simply collapsed. The house was still waiting for demolition. It hadn't occurred to her until now to consider other possibilities: the lot paved into a parking lot for the nearby dentist, or seeded over with those skeletal, malignant cottonwoods, or—worst of all—the house still there, as always.

Remodeled, fixed-up, the same clapboard box repainted and enlarged. It unnerved her to think of lights on in the windows, people mutely speaking inside, an empty car running in the driveway.

Lynn noticed her mother was staring at her.

"Were you so unhappy, Lynn?" Now her mother was impatient, moving on ahead.

"No, Mom."

"Did all those Girl Scout meetings and pets and toys, did they, what, scar you somehow?" Her mother glanced back once, pulling her beanie down over her ears like a lost little kid. Her filmy gray eyes were huge. "Why do you always act like you were a victim of us? Oh, honey. I love you, I do, but I refuse to say *poor girl*."

*

A few weeks after Thanksgiving, Lynn's brother called. They talked for a while about collies and taxes, about a bus strike in a distant city. It often surprised Lynn that this restrained, educated man was once her little brother. It embarrassed her to think how he was once almost a part of her body: the brother part, that went everywhere she did.

Just as Lynn was preparing to say goodbye, Saul added, bashfully, "Mom's upset. She thinks you're keeping something from us."

Us. She wanted to punish him for working against her. She wanted to remind him that he was hers, the brother part of her body. But when she opened her mouth, a sound like a sob came out.

"Lynn?"

"Fuck off, Saul, for once!" she said. Then, quickly, "No, no. I'm sorry. Listen." She wanted to offer him something, to be forgiven. She said, abruptly, "*I* killed the mice."

"What?"

"Midget and Dill." The names were absurd. She started to laugh.

"I thought I did that." She could hear in his voice the sound of a person stopping in his tracks and trying to get oriented. "I took them out of the cage and let them go when I was a little kid."

"That's what Mom told you!" It felt right to accuse her. "They got out on their own and lived under the refrigerator. They had babies and ate them."

"That's sick. I still dream about them all the time. I know how they felt when I lifted them out, how they struggled, and I squeezed their necks. I remember everything."

He sounded so bleak, so remorseful.

"You were just a kid, Sauly!" she reassured him. "You didn't know any better!"

There was a pause. "But you just said I didn't do anything."

Lynn put one palm against her mouth to keep from arguing. She lifted it up to say, "Yeah, well—" then put it back, very neatly. She felt confused, now, and distrustful of Saul, who talked secretly to their mother after Lynn was gone, who was the true favorite, the beloved son, who believed everything he was told.

*

When her mother died, Lynn was in bed with a man who refused to make love to her unless she begged for it, unless she put her hands on his dick and said *please, please*. Her sister made the call, and when Lynn's lover answered the phone, he said, "Wait a second—" He fumbled over Lynn, found his glasses on the nightstand, and then said into the phone, "Alrighty, then." Lynn could hear her sister's voice through the phone, her impatience with this man she did not know. She could hear in her sister's voice how much she resented Lynn this performance of politeness with a stranger. Lynn took the receiver and spoke to her sister for less than two minutes. She heard her lover flush the toilet in the bathroom. When she hung up the phone, there was a brief, blind moment when his face fled her mind. She couldn't feel the bed beneath her or her hands squeezing her thighs. She couldn't fathom who would come out of the bathroom when the door opened up. Then she remembered and he came out.

*

"The library only had books with creamy leather covers," she said. "There was a wingback chair in the corner with worn arms and a single brass lamp. And there were these old portraits of people on the walls, total strangers. Gilded frames, frowning faces. Three whole walls were covered floor to ceiling with books. Their spines creaked when you opened them up, and the words were in written in this tiny, elegant font. Like every book was a Bible. But listen. If you pulled a book from any shelf all the other books shifted to fill in the space it had left. There were never any gaps."

"My room was the conservatory." Henna was sipping red wine from a glass. They were in the basement of their childhood church, sitting at a long folding table. It had been afternoon not long ago, but now it was night. All the coifed cousins and hunched uncles had already left to scrape ice from their windshields and beat rush-hour traffic. Lynn and Henna and Saul were waiting for their father to finish signing papers in the church office.

"Your room?" Lynn asked, confused. Her own wine glass was empty.

"You're talking about that game we used to play, right? When, like, we were all crammed together in the backseat, stuck in traffic. Tearing into each other."

"I don't remember any game."

"'You get one room to yourself,' Mom would say. 'And no one else can ever come inside. What room is it you want?' She did it to stop us from squabbling. I said conservatory because I liked that room in Clue. Mom said kitchen, of course, and Saul—? Sauly, you weren't born yet, were you?" Henna looked over at Saul, who was sitting blank-faced on a column of folding chairs he had just stacked. His beard was damp. His long white fingers were splayed out over his knees.

Lynn shook her head. "That's not—"

"I was born," Saul said.

Henna was giggling, tipsy. "Lynn always said library, library, library."

"I was born!" Saul said, more loudly.

"It was a game?" It was a *dream*. Lynn felt uneasy now. And worried that Saul might be crying silently to himself, and irritated with Henna for getting drunk. Why couldn't they ever pat each other's hands or tell stupid jokes, offer some measure of consolation? It unsettled her that she couldn't call up a single image of them all sitting together in the backseat of some car, stuck in traffic. She tried but couldn't remember her shoulders touching Henna's and Saul's, couldn't remember the drumbeat bass from another car's radio, couldn't recall Saul's sticky little arm elbowing hers, or Henna kicking her legs out across Lynn's lap. She couldn't remember it and then, like waking from a dream itself, she did— of course, she *did*—their mother whipping around from the front seat, her face tired but trying as she suggested her game, and everyone groaning when their father said *bed*. Shelter, the game was called. Their mother's game.

"Saul was born," Lynn whispered.

"I was, I was," he said.

She lurched across the table to touch his arm as he sobbed.

He shirked away from her reaching hand. Even so, his bearded child's face was so hopeful, and so stricken, that it seemed possible to Lynn for a brief instant that no other reality had in fact ever fully existed for any of them, that there had only ever been that old car on the highway with all of them inside, each locked in their chosen rooms, and she wondered in anguish and awe how many times she would forget and have to remember this again.

LOCK JAW

My wife has taken to her bed, and though she isn't there always, she's there pretty often. Good days, she wears the slippers Jeremy picked out for her at Christmas. When she puts these on, I know how hard she's trying. They're pterodactyls. They have four fuzzy wings.

She says being in bed at five makes her feel rich, and who am I to disagree? It's true, I've made a lot of money in recent years writing about lunatics and apocalypse. I wrote one novel about a man who gets chased by a demon monkey, and it was made into a movie, which was never officially released. But mysteriously—miraculously—I saw a trailer for it once, on TV in the middle of the night. The demon monkey wore a more helpless expression than I'd ever imagined for it, like a calf's or a child's.

"Are you feeling any better?" my wife asks. I've just gotten back from getting dinner.

"A little, yes," I tell her. I've had a cold, and though it's gone now, I continue to dab my nose and hold one hand to my chest. This makes us both feel better.

The fried rice stands in a carton-shaped tower on the plate when I hand it to her. She takes it. "Did you go out without a hat? I can't be your mom, Craig. I can't." But she's already smiling up at me. She's always had a flexible face, and now more than ever I can see each word move across it in a little wave. Sometimes I think I can see a word before she says it in the squint around her eyes. Like now. Like how she starts to say, *No thanks,* but stops herself.

"This looks great." She separates her wooden chopsticks with a crack, and then uses them to lift puckered peas from the brick of rice one by one. "But Charlotte won't take a bite if she sees these. Help me out?"

"That's not eating," I warn her.

"*You* eat them." She sticks a pea in my face.

I open my mouth.

"The kids'll get dropped off at six, and—" She hesitates. "The dog got out." She gives me a look like, *I told you this would happen,* then turns back to the plate. I can see how reluctant she is to ruin the tower of rice, how she plucks out only the peas on the sides, the most accessible. She spends a long time on a single pea wedged in the brick's corner.

"Fuck," I say, finally.

She sighs. With her free hand, she adjusts the wig on her head. "I don't know how it happened, honestly. There was some kind of scuffle at the door when the kids were leaving this morning. You'll have to go look for her before it gets dark."

It's already dark. I unlock my bike from the back porch railing and step onto the pedals, balancing them against each other for a second—just standing—before leaning on my right foot and bearing down. I squint because it's snowing. Once, when I was a kid, I fell off my bike and busted up my face so bad I needed stitches from eye to scalp. In the past few months, I always think of that when the wheels first turn, before I really get going. I'd begged to stay home from school, and my dad had said, *But that's how you get ahead!* How? *By lowering people's expectations.*

Now, as I pedal down the street, fast, I see all the neighbors have wandered out to their driveways. They hold their shovels in the air like weapons, like pitchforks. Why do they always want so badly for flurries to turn into drifts? They're from the city, mostly—ex-lawyers, new hippies—and they keep chickens in their backyards as pets. In the summer they plant the dreariest plants, sweet corn and rutabaga. We don't live in the country, exactly, but in a kind of woods on the edge of the city's last suburbs, and as I bike down the street I call for the dog, which reassures everyone. The neighbors get worried when they see a grown man riding around alone on his bike. They probably think I'm a pervert or something, so it's nice for them that I have a reason to be out like this.

"Renee!" I shout. But not very hopefully.

One of the neighbors waves at me as I pass. "Lost dog? Can I help?" he asks, raising his shovel up in a do-goody kind of way.

"Thanks!" I say, meaning *no*, but he misunderstands, I suppose, because when I turn the corner, I can hear him behind me taking up my call. Going, "Renee! Renee! Renee!" as if some sweetheart of his has closed her door and won't come out for him. As if Renee were his one true love.

A mastiff's mouth exerts 320 pounds of pressure per square inch. That's what my brother tells me. My brother has been coming by a lot, lately, with these books in pastel jackets and red candles in glass domes. He's always been a lonely bastard. Sometimes when I'm locking up my bike in the backyard, I can see him sitting with my wife on our bed, their silhouettes against the bedroom blinds like shadow puppets. It's all too staged, too obvious to talk about. When I go inside, he's in socks. He has a book in his lap, he's reading to her. Somewhere along the line, my wife found God, but not the Catholic one she grew up with.

My brother reads things like: "It is when we try to make our will conform with God's that we begin to use it rightly."

He reads: "Our whole trouble had been the misuse of will-power. We had tried to bombard our problems with it instead of attempting to bring it into agreement with God's intention for us."

My wife looks up whenever I come into the room, but my brother never does. He just keeps on reading to the end of the paragraph, doing each word like it's a full sentence, blinking his eyes slowly like an owl. My dad used to call him a pussyfooter because he was late for everything and wouldn't get his fingers dirty. I remember he once let his hamster cage go black with shit before he dumped it out, hamster and all, in the woods. I still felt sorry for him then. I remember rocking our bunk bed like a boat when he wouldn't sleep, pushing the wooden frame away from the wall. *There was a ghost ship*, I told him. *There was a boy without hands*. But my father was right. When my brother finishes the paragraph, he closes his book by bringing together his two palms on either side of the cover. He says things like, "We'll meditate on that."

He thinks my wife needs him now. He went to Arizona and found a version of God he thinks is compatible with my wife's sorrow. He drives my children to choir practice. Buckles them in place, adjusts the rearview mirror.

Dogs aren't stupid, my brother tells me, but they judge objects first by their movements, then their brightness, *then* their shape. He says the order is the opposite for humans, which is what makes dogs so dangerous. *And so discerning*, I think.

For instance. Renee always lifts her blue upper lip at the Jehovah's Witness who comes by with her bucolic pictures of lions licking lambs. Renee knows that lady's fooling no one, that she's just looking for occasions to feel superior. Or another example. Once Charlotte's friend's mother came in the front door, wiped her feet on the carpet, and said, "I must have stepped in *something* in the yard." When her daughter, Charlotte's friend, asked to spend the night, what that woman said to me was, "Oh, but you don't have a mat."

What she meant was that we didn't pick up after our dog often enough. That we didn't grow wholesome rutabaga in our backyard or volunteer for the PTA. She meant, *No, you can't stay here with them.*

Charlotte stared down at the doll in her arms like it had died. She was eight.

That's when Renee came in the room, her head lowered. By then she was almost two hundred pounds and had a blunt-wedge face like a piece of armor. Her sound was more purr than growl. "Put your hands behind your back," I said.

That woman in her heels went, "Excuse me?"

I loved watching her go white, and then red, the bits of skin around her hair getting blotchy.

I said, "Just be careful with your movements. Don't look the dog in the eye."

Then I added, kindly, "But don't be too anxious either. Anxiety's just as bad."

We all watched as Renee's black hackles rose and fell again, a bristly wave.

My wife has been thinking ahead. She says she worries what will happen when our children are old enough to stumble on and read *The Trilogy of Leviathan's Children.* She wants me to put the books on high shelves. She wants me to put them behind other books.

I oblige her for now, feeling with a pang just how easy it is to agree to things when you know they're temporary.

It's true I've always told her I was a hack. So it would be hard to explain to my wife that there's something in those books I'm proud of, in fact, something I'd like the kids to see. When I first started writing, I gave the characters my favorite names, which years later became the names of our children. Jeremiah Peter, for instance, was the protagonist in my second book. And our Charlotte was first Ms. Charlotta Linkley Grey, an Australian obstetrician who finds herself pregnant with one third of a baby—the other two thirds of which (the torso, three limbs) are in distant women's bodies. These three women live through the apocalypse and have to coordinate the birth with drugs and stitch the parts of the baby together. It's an elaborate, ghastly surgery. It's not a metaphor, it's just the end of the world.

I'm not really superstitious. I don't believe in luck or prophecy, so it's weird to me to see how much of Charlotta Linkley there is in my little girl. Of the three mothers, Charlotta is the only one unwilling to give her child up for science, even when her third of the infant almost dies, even when the head and shoulders separate from the torso while she's nursing.

Charlotte is mad about her dollhouse. Every day she empties out all of its furniture, makes a pile on the floor of all the chairs and beds. The rugs like potholders, the pots like thimbles. She tells her little brother, "You may choose one room and four pieces of furniture to survive with." He's five. He wants the attic, of course, which is the highest room in the house, but she always chooses the bathroom because it has a water source and only one door to guard.

"Guard against what?" Jeremy asked her once.

I could see she thought about not telling him. "People outside," she said.

My wife says she's concerned about Charlotte because, since the incident last fall at Renee's obedience class, she no longer invites her friends over to play. "She used to be so popular," my wife complains. "Where are all her friends now?"

My wife blames me for this. I blame her for blaming me.

But since she gave notice at work, we've both gotten pretty good at choosing words that leave no marks. We interact with utmost politeness, and it has been surprising to me that all this niceness isn't cold, the way I always assumed nice people to be. It's delicate, yes, but also tender. We used to have fights so fierce that when my wife uncrossed her arms I saw red marks where her fingers had been. Who would have thought that all we needed all along was a certain mutual commitment to circumspection?

Now when she worries, I take her thin hand. I try to reassure her.

"But look at Charlotte," I told her recently. "She's still *happy*, see?" I meant it.

We stood together in the doorway of the children's bedroom and watched our daughter wipe down her tiny porcelain tub with a tissue. She was waiting for Jeremy to come back from the real bathroom, rocking back and forth on her knees, petting the hair under her ponytail. For her furniture, she chose a stove, one pot, a mattress, and a cake.

When he came back, Jeremy took the four dolls. It was a family of bears, all wearing dresses and hats.

"That's not furniture!" Charlotte yelled, when she realized what he was doing. But what she was really mad about was that there wasn't anyone left to survive in her bathroom. She menaced him: "What will they eat? Where will they sleep?"

Charlotte hates it when people won't play by the rules, or when they change them in any way. Like when I said I wouldn't be driving her to choir practice anymore, that Uncle Brady would do it. When Charlotte heard this, she led Renee by one velvet ear into the closet. She wouldn't come out until I dumped out the dollhouse and chose a room. "I want the solarium," I said, adding, "and this chair which is also a bed, and this magical pot that is a toilet and fire pit and fishbowl and a pillow all in one."

"That's not *fair*," she cried. "You can't use magic." But out she came.

Or like when Charlotte walks the dog, and Jeremy is supposed to go in front and be on the lookout for animals. Other dogs, squirrels, cats, small children. But one night just before the first snowfall, Charlotte came home with blood glittering up and down her arm and a bubble of saliva before every word. "He didn't do his *job*," she sobbed. "He was kicking a *rock* and didn't tell me about the raccoon."

"Why didn't you just let go of the leash?" I asked her, pulling strands of hair out of her mouth one by one. She'd been dragged across the parking lot on her stomach. Her chin was bleeding. Her jacket was torn.

She looked confused. She said she hadn't thought of that.

That night I told Jeremy I would read him a book. I watched him pick one out across the room and head for the spot next to me on the couch. Then, eyeing Renee sprawled near my feet, he stopped and changed course. He made a wide circle around the coffee table and approached the couch from behind, throwing himself over the upholstered back. He fell dead-man style onto a cushion. "Umph," he said.

I took him in my arms and put my face in his hair. He smelled like a baby, still. Like milk and sleep, like urine.

"Jeremy," I whispered in his ear. "Are you afraid of Renee?"

We watched her lift her heavy head, turn to face us. She pulled herself up on her huge haunches, a pearl of mucus shining in each black eye. Jeremy wouldn't say a word.

"Dogs can see if you're afraid," I told him. "*Act* as if you trust her."

It was good advice. My son hasn't yet learned to differentiate his actions from his thoughts, which makes him unpredictable. I can't tell if this is because he isn't old enough yet to do this, or if it is a flaw in his personality. Once, when his mother asked him to play Go Fish with her in bed, he refused, saying she looked funny. This made her cry. I had Jeremy apologize to her that night, and he said—with a sincerity that was all the more cruel for its artlessness—"I'm sorry you look funny, Mom."

Whenever I get home early from a meeting, I make sure to bring my brother his shoes from the front door. I tiptoe through the house to the back bedroom, dangling his sometimes sodden sneakers on two hooked fingers. It's humiliating in ways I can't describe, but I hate seeing him in his socks with my wife, and I want him to leave. Sometimes I stand in the dark hallway before I enter, watching him say "principle of all being" like he's only just now learned to sound out words, and I think about chucking the shoes and clocking him in the back of the head. I never do this, of course. While my brother leans over to tie his wet laces, my wife tells me to feed him anything he wants—chicken, coffee, noodles. She wants him to be fed; she wants me to be nicer to him.

"I *know* what you're thinking," she whispered to me once, late at night, long after I had thought she'd fallen asleep. "But you know better than to tell that tired adultery story to yourself, even in your head. Don't even start. Look at me. Look at you. We *need* him."

I tend to give him food in wrappers so he can take it with him. Popsicles, Capri Suns, granola bars. It makes me feel better to watch him struggle with the sticky plastic wrapper on a Fruit Roll-Up. He licks his fingers like a five-year-old, has gummy red slugs between his teeth.

"Everything okay with you?" he always asks on the way to the door. I swear to God, he squints his eyes. He looks at me like I'm an experiment, like he wants to prod me with a stick or something, even though he's the one with a scarlet mouth stained by Red Dye No. 2.

Once, as he was stepping around the dog at the threshold, Renee sprang up from her sleep and seized his sneaker. It happened so fast. For a moment I thought he was shouting at me because I hadn't answered his question, hadn't said whether I was okay. I started shouting back before I realized he was kicking my dog.

"That's what I'm saying!" he told me when we got outside. I could see his pulse distorting his neck, going under his skin like a little burrowing bug. He rolled up the leg of his pants and tenderly pressed his shin. The skin wasn't even broken, just dented where teeth had pressed down. "Dogs like that have lockjaws, Craig. I'm *not* making this up. You need to pry open their jaws when they bite down hard, which is not something you want to get messed up with."

"Bullshit," I said.

He was furious, and then—in that flip he can do with his emotions, like wiping a chalkboard—he calmed down. He shoved a sleeve of blond hair back from his eyes. He climbed into the driver's seat of my car. "Believe what you want."

I wondered that night after he left, where the fuck did he get this stuff? Even as a child, he was always reading everything he could get his hands on—cereal boxes, Hardy Boys books, comic books, encyclopedias—because he had no sense of imagination. It was like he could make nothing up on his own; he couldn't care less about the games we invented on the playground. The problem with my brother was that he had no ability to hold two realities in his mind at once, the hypothetical and the concrete, so he conflated the two. Which made him paranoid in his teenage years, afraid of murderers and weather and germs, unwilling to leave the house for a full month when he was thirteen. Dad got really pissed at him, and I'd have to coax him from his room at night with a frozen lasagna. At some point around then, he starting washing his hands so many times a day, the floor of our bathroom stayed damp all the time. A strange kind of mold grew up between the tiles, and it was too green to be normal, and I didn't like to look at it.

According to the new schedule, my brother picks us up at nine on Sundays. Because it's my wife's new church we're going to I've started letting her sit in front. Last week, I sat in the backseat between Charlotte and Jeremy, who were quiet and stiff as statues—Charlotte, because she was wearing a new dress, something my wife's church acquaintance had given her. It was calico and shapeless, with a stained lace apron sewed on the front. Charlotte was thinking of herself as a pioneer on a prairie. I could see it in the way she crossed her hands over her lap and whispered to herself about *Ma* and *Pa*. She murmured, "Pa says we've *got* to go into town," and it dawned on me that Pa was the one up front, the one driving this carriage. She wanted Jeremy to hold her pretend cat, and when he wouldn't, she handed it to me. "Okay, Brother Baker?" she asked. I wondered, *Who the hell is that?* But I obliged, reluctantly, putting one hand on either side of empty space.

Jeremy was silent because he was upset about what had happened before we left. He'd refused to get in the car. He'd pulled off his good shirt—in a sleight-of-body gesture that looked more bird than human—and wailed, "I don't want to go to church!" loud enough for his mother in the car to hear him. When I said, "Stop it!" he'd run out of the garage and into the front yard. He threw his shirt into the street. I took off after him, tackled him when he dove into the bristly dead grass, wrestled him into my body. I got his scrawny bare arms locked over his chest and hissed, "You need to go to church for Mommy. She's sick, so she gets to say. Got that, buster?"

I took Renee to just that one obedience class in September. That was after she broke through the screen and chased the UPS man, who threatened to report her. Renee sat on command and heeled like a pro, everyone said so. Her choke collar clinked loosely as jewelry around her neck. For Leave It we were the class model; everyone stood in a circle and watched. But then, when I did the thing where you unclasp the leash and take ten steps back, when I did that and said, "Come!" Renee tore after this little white rug of a dog and got it by the neck. In the car on the way home, Renee sat panting in the front seat. Charlotte was squeezed between Renee and the door, her pale little arms draped over Renee's massive shoulders. It had been Charlotte who'd known what to do, in class, who'd jumped up from her folding chair and thrown herself on Renee. She'd kicked that floppy little dog away like a champ.

But she'd heard, afterward, what the trainer had said about Renee. *One more incident like this and she'll have to be put down.* In the car, Charlotte clung helplessly to the dog. Renee ignored her completely.

"We'll just have to keep her away from danger," I said. "Keep her away from other dogs and strangers." My fingers were shaking. I couldn't keep them in their plastic grooves on the steering wheel. The windshield wipers kept going, *shush, shush, shush,* and there was something oddly thrilling about that, as if Charlotte and Renee and I were all in on a secret.

"I'm so afraid," Charlotte said, her arms around the dog. "I'm so afraid."

"You're pretending to love God," my wife accused me recently.

This was after my brother caught me sleeping in church. He'd nudged me awake, saying in his wheedling, self-righteous voice, "Come on, Craig. Be a little more respectful." I'd stood up then and walked out. I'd had to press past a dozing old woman, waking her up, and Jeremy, who was on the floor with trucks.

I didn't have the keys to the car, so I sat on the cold metal hood and bounced the whole thing down and up. After a minute, my brother came out, jacketless. He was wearing gloves, though, black leather. He stood a few feet away and clapped his leathered hands together, saying, "I'm not, I'm really not, working against you, man."

I thought about that. I thought about all the stories I used to tell him at night—the armless boys, the ghost ships, everything. I gave him everything good of mine I could think of because, for reasons no one could account for, he always seemed to have so little.

"You feel better, now?" I asked him, bouncing down hard on the hood. "You like your new car? It gets good mileage, right? And it's nice to have a family, a wife, even if she's—"

"Don't." He put two leather hands together. Pulled them apart. "Don't what?"

He gave me a look like when he'd come home when we were kids and I'd dismantled the bunk bed. "What *step* you on, Craig? Is this one of the steps?"

"Get off my back."

After he dropped us all off at home, the kids stayed in their jackets in the living room, Charlotte roping herself over the dog and watching some orchestral cartoon violence on TV. At some point I noticed she was sweating. Her hair was damp around her ears. Jeremy sat with his sleeves pushed up, humming and sucking his thumb, arranging the dollhouse furniture in an elaborate free-standing tower.

My wife called me into our bedroom, and her hands were cold when she touched my cheeks. She said she wanted her slippers. There was something in her voice that climbed stairs, that got so much higher than me suddenly.

"Are you pretending?" she asked, when I pushed one of her feet into the plush insides of the pterodactyl. "Will you stop all this?" She wouldn't say *when I'm gone.*

"All what?"

She closed her eyes. "You know. Going to church, doing your meetings."

I slid her other foot into the slipper, pushing my hand in too and leaving it there a moment. I lay my head against her knee. *Of course I am,* I thought.

I'm pretending to love God because I really love her, and isn't that good? Isn't that good enough?

I decide to circle back past the house. The snow is coming down in gusts, dragging over parked cars and pulling things off the ground. Dead leaves do a miniature cyclone over a gutter. An orange garage sale sign sails past, kite-like, weirdly lovely. All the neighbors have gone inside except the one I talked to when I first set out, the one who keeps at it like a dirge. "Reneee! Reneee! Reneee!" I can't stand to pass by that man again, so I take the long way home, behind the school. The tires of my bike roll smoothly over the new snow, then stop rolling and slide, and then start rolling again. As I near the house, I think I see someone in the front yard playing in the snow. That's what it looks like from a block away, like someone rolling those balls to make igloos, or flapping their arms around, angel-style. And then I realize it's Renee I'm watching. Renee, come home all on her own. She's rolling joyously, thrashing something, and it's only because I've stopped watching the ground in front of me that the tires slip. I fall sideways into a freshly plowed bank, but the landing is so soft, so forgiving. It doesn't feel like falling.

"Renee!" I say, with a surge of relief, as the dog gets up and runs toward me, and I open my arms to catch her. There's snow everywhere. She seems to be crying.

I hear Charlotte calling the dog inside and slamming the door.

I realize then it's Jeremy, not Renee, I have in my arms. He seems barely more substantial than the wet clothes he's wearing. He must be half, a third, of Renee's weight. Less than that even. "Dad!" he sobs.

There's something I always think of when I'm trying to quiet Jeremy down, when Charlotte's knocked his tower over, or when I'm putting him to bed. I'll be arranging the blankets, telling him the kinds of stories he likes, the ones with bees, but in another part of my mind, I'm thinking about Jeremiah Peter Black. Jeremiah Peter is from a race of parapsychic men. He lives in the aftermath of the apocalypse, a few years after Charlotta Grey, and because he's smart, it doesn't take long for Jeremiah to understand that it was his mind, and people with minds like his, that caused the disaster—that by a sheer accident of nightmarish daydreaming, knives had drifted up off of tables into people's necks. Whole forests burned to stumpy trunks, and rivers ran crimson. In his grief, in his unrelenting, dry-mouthed guilt, Jeremiah Peter Black creates a new sect, a priesthood called Control Thought, and every day he trains himself in his pile of potshards to think of fruit trees and libraries and canned soup. He falls in love, grows old, trains doe-eyed pupils to lick their empty palms and taste sugar.

The world rebuilds, and Jeremiah sees it all with satisfaction. And yet, he senses behind each well-intentioned thought the shadow he veers away from, the torch, the gleaming knife, the explosion of light, and just as he congratulates himself on avoiding these things, they appear of course—the old crumbling world coming alive again, in which everything is a skull—and he sees with horror how the shadow eats its source, and so his own cells disintegrate, piece by piece, mitochondria by leaf, brick by fingertip, until there is nothing left.

That's not a good story. When my wife finished *Shepherd of the Deep*, she wouldn't speak to me for a whole day. But I don't think it was because she was mad. She was twenty-six that year, and I remember for Christmas she sewed me a quilt with fluffy white clouds and mountains, a brook. We made love under that quilt. But the book did poorly. It sold only sold nine hundred copies, and I never read it again after it was done. I may even be remembering it wrong.

Jeremy clings to me, sobbing.

I say, "You alright?"

They'd made a snowman, he tells me.

He pulls back, pushing a piece of mangled skin over his eyes with two fingers. Blood pours down his face.

He adds, bawling, "Renee ruined it!"

His snot is pink, then bright red. His mittens have come off and they dangle by silver clips from his wrists. When I lift him up, I swear, he floats. I feel like I've tossed him in the air and I need to catch hold of him again before he gets away. I pull him down and onto my back, because he's my son and I will not call my brother now. I will not. I say to him, "Can you hold on?" and though he doesn't answer, I know he will. As I go down the road on my bike, I am very, very careful. I'm as careful as I've ever been. My fingers fit the grooves in the handlebars, each finger in its place, and the tires hold the road. The hospital is two miles away, and the whole way there, I feel his arms around my neck, his breath in my ear. The snow comes down so hard there isn't any sound.

We've been to Saint Vincent's so many times with his mom, Jeremy is almost bored with it. He won't be distracted by toys. He wants the nurses to talk to him. After I've filled out the paperwork at the desk, I go back into the drab little room where they've taken him for his stitches. In the doorway, I hear a nurse with inch-long red fingernails say to him, touching her own face, "What happened? What brought you here, honey?"

I freeze. But he misunderstands the question. "On the bike."

There's a pause while the nurse is nodding. Jeremy goes on explaining, moving from effect to cause the way he does, working his way backward. "The police said to stop driving the car. Daddy was too funny with the beer. That was way before Halloween."

I'm surprised by how much he knows, but only for a moment, because the surprise itself makes the moment unreal, almost exciting, and I am released the way you are when you hear a bad story about someone else, or get to a sad part in a book that you've long been expecting. I wait for a feeling that doesn't come. And then the nurse says, "What?" and anything might happen, but nothing does, because as I go into the room I sense in a rush that Jeremy's mistake about her question might also be a lucky break. I learned long ago how important it is to capitalize on misunderstandings. In the moment before the nurse turns around, before I gather up Jeremy in my arms, I think of how we first found Renee. I think of how Charlotte opened the car door after I thought I'd hit something along the road—how I'd driven off the shoulder again, and there was a bump so I slowed—and this huge creature had leapt into the backseat. She was indifferent to us, wet with snow, unharmed. I could have cried. It had been like being forgiven everything.

I say to the nurse at Saint Vincent's, letting my voice be angry for a second, "There's some goddamn loose dog on the streets. What can you do?"

The nurse looks pained, takes her claw-like hand and puts it against her chest.

I lift Jeremy up and put him on my back again, and he does not complain. He fits perfectly. On the ride home, I ask into the wind, "You okay, Little Bullfrog?" He says his eye hurts, but only when he opens it.

I tell him then we're going to have a secret. I tell him we need to be careful what we say around Mommy because we all love Renee, him and Charlotte and me, and she didn't mean to be bad. I make myself clear. "Listen," I say. "We have to tell Mommy something else, it was your bike that did it, you fell, and we have to tell her that because she's sick right now. Got it?"

We bike toward our house in the snow. My son is just the right weight on my back, not too heavy, just heavy enough, and I almost don't want to slow down as we approach our driveway. It's too good a thing to carry around my son like this. I don't have to pedal for a moment, and we move in an effortless drift through tiny whips of fresh snow. There is no one now outside. All the neighbors have their evening programs to watch, or herbs to pot in their basements. Even the snowplow is just distant lights, a slow senseless blinking in another neighborhood altogether. We have the whole road to ourselves. It is only when we get closer to home that I see Charlotte standing there right inside the screen door, looking out. She's squinting suspiciously into the night, trying to tell what is what in the dark, and Renee looms beside her—statuesque, surreal, guard against all evil—and so I lean the bike against the railing and lift up my son and we go inside.

TIME DIFFERENCE

"It's raining in Hollywood." Her brother's voice skips notes.

"It *is* raining," she tells him over the phone. "That's some magic you have there, the Internet." When his silence sails past comfortable, she adds, "Everything okay in the Dairy State?"

"Why are you asking?" His voice is pentatonic, black-keyed.

"It's pretty late—"

"It's just after eleven!"

"Okay, okay," she soothes.

For a moment she thinks he's right, there's nothing wrong. And she feels bad for her chastising tone, for wanting off the phone, until she remembers he's obscured an important point that establishes their distance.

"My time it's almost midnight," she tells him. "Your time it's nearly two."

*

Her mother on the phone the next morning is apologetic. "Did I wake you up?"

"Well—" She pours coffee to clear her head and sits down in front of the window, out of which she sees two doves nicking and fluffing each other with beaks. They're perched on a wet wire, and every time they touch, the whole thing drips across the yard.

"How're you doing? Did you say you've been volunteering?"

"Yeah." She holds the mug on her knee, feeling the warmth spread through her from that one point. She's proud of her good intentions and worried at the same time that they're just that, with no underlying fact of generosity. She tells her mother, "It's nothing. I haven't really started yet. I just finished training."

The birds outside lift the feathers on their necks like hackles: now doves, now tiny spiked predators. Her neighbor in his yellow car has flooded his engine trying to get it started. It occurs to her, suddenly, that her mother must have forgotten the time difference, too, or else why would she call so early on a Friday morning? "I'm a little groggy. I'm sorry, Mom. You know, it's still pretty early here."

"Your brother's in jail."

"Okay." She closes her eyes, opens them.

She tries to think about how he sounded last night on the phone, whether she knew and ignored what's obvious when she looks back on it. But the doves shimmy across the wire, and her mind drifts. While she's thinking about how she used to call her brother from a friend's house when they were kids, while she's thinking about how she used to say, "The Wizard's coming for you," and how thrilled her little brother had been, how terrified, while she's thinking about how it seemed like she was blessing him at the time, but how her pleasure might also have come from succeeding in the lie, her mother tells her about her brother's second DWI. Then, without any noticeable transition, her mother starts talking about her own father, who died in 1957 on a wheat farm in Texas. She explains the difference between summer wheat and winter wheat, how the latter sprouts with the first freeze and then lies dormant till spring.

"I'm not sure what you're trying to say, Mom."

"Everyone was always saying it was icy. It was an icy morning in the wheat fields. But now I wonder if it wasn't an easier thing to say than he was drunk again and that's why he crashed."

"What are you going to do, Mom?"

"What *am* I going to do? Tell me that." Her mother is in her fifties, widowed, loyal to horoscopes. She is afraid of making decisions that work against her fate.

The doves rear and carve open their wings, settle back.

Her mother sighs. "I guess what you're saying is that I have to go pick him up?"

*

She rinses her mug and overturns it on the rack, wondering as she does whether she's ever seen ice in Texas. As a child, whenever she'd taken the two-day car trip down I-35 to visit her grandmother, the cramped Texas house was always sunk in a marvelous kind of heat. She and her brother sat very still in front of the muted TV, drained even of boredom. It is hard for her to imagine that house covered in snow, a cold morning, a crash of any sort.

In Hollywood, drizzle mottles the windows.

She goes back to the bedroom, where her boyfriend slugs out of the covers. Without his glasses, he has an amphibian look, his eyes all innocence. "Jill?" he asks. She knows she'll have to get very close before he can read her expression, so she stays for a moment in the doorway and watches him.

"Who was that? Is there something wrong?"

She snorts to snuff out an unexpected sob. "My mom has a theory about my grandfather's death."

"She called for that? Come back to bed for a few minutes."

It pours. Like an optical trick, the windows shimmer with water just as the clouds open up. Sun refracts through the room, and the day feels, abruptly, like another day altogether. Like the afternoon on a weekend after a holiday, all the presents opened, nothing in the world left to want. "Don't we have jobs?" she asks him. "Aren't we going to be late?"

He lifts his glasses, returns his face to its proper shape. "Shit. What time is it?"

The sun makes the room instantly hot. She feels like squinting. "Almost eight. But I need to get to work early so I can leave early tonight. Did you forget?" She feels irritable about the possibility that he has, and that's a relief. It's good to have a specific, sensible source for anger. She glares at him and hopes he sees it. "Don't forget, please? Today is the fifteenth. Friday. We're meeting Manny and her husband what's-his-name for dinner."

*

She showers quickly and rushes out, but once on the highway she leans back and lets the car drift through traffic. A carcass on the road turns out to be a palm frond. The exit ramp is strewn with lemon-yellow leaves. She gets off the highway early and takes the side roads toward the hills. She doesn't, in fact, have to work until noon. They've cut back her hours at the lab, where she harvests cells with a razor blade from the scalps of rats. When she tells people about her job, it sounds more ghoulish than it is, less mind-numbing and banal. She doesn't mind working less. She's been filling the extra time by volunteering at a public-school program for homeless families. She teaches reading and math to Angelo, who's shy and ten and moves clumsily, like a fat boy, though he's *not* fat. Just big for his age. She likes him a lot. She thinks of him fondly as she parks the car and trots through the metal gates at the door, as she smooths and signs the smudged register there—right up until the moment she sees him lumbering up to her in the school's conference room. Then, unaccountably, she feels dismay. His hair curls wetly down his neck. His mouth is bulging with something.

She finds herself saying, sternly, "No candy, Angelo, while we're working."

Out of his mouth slides something glistening and larval, with points. It lands with a wet plop on his math book.

Angelo grins.

"Is that an airplane?" she asks, incredulous.

*

The rats are smart, actually. No one gives enough credit to rats. When she first took the job, her colleagues at the lab made fun of her for naming them. They were hard to tell apart, the main difference being that some had a crop of pebbly tumors on their skulls, and some didn't. "Harvest" is what she does to them. After nine years of higher education, she is a farmer like her grand-pa was. But even without names—even bristly, corn-like in her hands—the rats are smart. She tries to remember that. She has to remember to bolt down the tops of their cages so they don't escape and chew open the cages across the lab and feast on the mice. When that happened last summer, two separate experiments were ruined, two multimillion-dollar grants from two different federal institutions. That's when her hours were cut back and her status as a lab technician changed to questionably proficient.

*

Angelo's math book is stained with saliva from the toy airplane. She suggests they read instead. She pulls out a book about witches, about magic and trolls, but he points instead to a book that de-scribes each and every kind of truck with an insidious level of de-tail. They've read this book before. Dump truck. Bulldozer. Tractor.

There is no story. But because she thinks of herself as good with children, she makes a story up. She says, "The suspicious tractor nursed a fear that he could not rid himself of his evil captor."

Angelo says, "Stop." He lifts his rounded shoulders. "The book doesn't *talk* like that."

"Sure, it does."

"Does *not*."

She is surprised by his intensity. He almost never crosses her, barely even talks. But now this large, black-haired child has pulled his arms inside his T-shirt and seems to be glaring at her. Each of his eyelashes looks separate and knowing, like the antennae of something that should crawl away.

She pours out her voice cheerfully, reads every tedious detail. She reads about earth movers and military scrapers and snow-plows, but she can't help adding just one little elf on principle—on the theory that she can teach Angelo how to be a child, poor kid—and Angelo, fed up, crawls under the table. He takes off his shoes and builds a wall between them. He adds to the wall his backpack, a Transformers lunch box, and a plastic goat.

She feels, out of proportion, hurt, and yet, for reasons she can't understand, she goes on relentlessly reading. "The elf was friends with the Great Wizard, who was a kind of God. Some trucks were under His control and were magic, and the other trucks were just trucks."

*

In the car on the way to dinner that night, she gets into a fight with her boyfriend. They don't fight often, but when they do, the fights descend upon them, elaborate and unique as snowflakes. What they're arguing about, bewilderingly, is the National Park Service. She's seen a documentary. "America's best idea," she quotes. He says, cheerfully almost, "Catering to middle-class romantic no-tions of 'wilderness.'" She can't understand what his angle is, why he opposes birds and woods. She wants to go camping. She wants to have gone camping when she was a child.

"You've *been* to Yosemite!" she accuses him. "You washed your face in that stream."

"Is that what this is about?" He sounds surprised. "You want to go? We can go if you want to go."

She finds herself speaking very fast. "That's not the point. It's not *personal*. It's about democracy and human dignity. It's about every-body, regardless of who you are, getting to experience some little corner of wildness for themselves. Isn't that only fair?" she asks.

Rain makes the gray concrete black. She's pleased, then ashamed, by his hurt silence.

"We're lost," she says.

"We're turned around," he says.

*

The dinner begins poorly. The Thai restaurant is cave-like, window-less, lantern-lit. The tables are too close, so as they wind their way to their seats, they have to touch strangers hunched over plates and beg their pardon. By the time they sit down, Jill feels an over-whelming urge to apologize to everyone. She's nervous. "Sorry the place is so packed! I heard it was good, but maybe not!" Across the table sit Jill's boyfriend, her friend's husband, two of Jill's colleagues. She has invited people from work to ease the tension of meeting someone she hasn't seen in years, but now, ridiculously, she can't remember one of those coworkers' names. It's Anna and Somebody.

She does her best to look busy examining her napkin. It has been folded into a crane.

"Cool?" she says to Manny, who's sitting so close their elbows touch.

"Absolutely," her old friend assures her, glancing down at the menu. "There's nothing better than a really hot curry."

She smiles back, relieved. Manny's open-mouthed way of chewing edamame is endearingly familiar. Didn't she used to eat lico-rice like that? Didn't they used to sleep in the same bed every Saturday night? For a few minutes—after Jill finishes her first two beers and before the third one comes—the brilliant spices in her curry make her hands seem to pulse and everyone else across the table seem too far away to matter. She lets cold, cold water slide in little strokes down her throat. At some point Manny tells her, con-spiratorially, between bites, that she's pregnant. "It's like I'm some-body's spaceship, some little fetus driving me around! But he—" She nods at her husband across the table. "—doesn't understand."

Jill licks her burning lips. In a moment of exuberant clarity, she thinks she sees how the unfamiliar present of her friend connects to the past they once shared. She reminds Manny about the time they lined up their dolls behind her mother's car so she'd drive over them when she backed out. Jill's almost whispering, only half joking, swigging from her empty bottle.

"I don't remember that," her friend says. "That's creepy."

Jill looks at her. "We were in our anti-girl stage, remember? We despised all those papers we had to sign to get babies from *cabbages*. We wanted to be pioneers with rifles." She casts around for a way to remind her. "We thought it was a horrible injustice people hadn't yet developed signs to communicate more meaningfully with other species."

Of course it sounds like a joke. Manny laughs. She scoots her chair back, glistens resplendently with sweat.

Jill remembers then that Manny hasn't had any beers—obviously, she's pregnant. She's pushed out on that little one-man boat, and Jill is still on shore. Forlornly, she lifts her rumpled napkin from her lap, tries unsuccessfully to work it back into a crane.

"So," Manny says, too perkily. "What have *you* been doing lately?"

"Volunteering," Jill shrugs. "With a homeless kid." She has a rehearsed story for times like these, a humorous story about the lab and the bald rats she breeds, but she feels a sudden, pressing need to underscore her impersonal good intentions. Isn't she trying to help the homeless? Isn't she better because of that? "This kid's a little terror, actually." She finds herself exaggerating Angelo's behavior, making things up. "Today he threw a tantrum and ran around screaming obscenities. The F-word, worse than that. He put a toy airplane in his mouth and threatened to chew it up and swallow the bits. He's crazy."

"That sounds a lot like your brother as a kid." Manny must see something in Jill's face, because she puts a gentle hand on her sleeve. "But you were always so good at dealing with Ryan. I'm sure you're doing a great job."

Her boyfriend inserts himself in the conversation by reaching across the table with chopsticks. "Ryan? Was he a bad seed even when he was little?"

Manny's lips are oily. "Oh, no. Is Ryan *still* getting into trouble?"

Jill's boyfriend raises his eyebrows, defers to Jill, who's still working on her napkin crane.

"He's fine," she says, breezily. "He's got a job at FedEx, actually. He sends things."

*

Once, when she was twelve and her brother was five, he ran in a fury out of the house. He'd been angry that their mother had left for work, furious that his Tonka truck had a bad wheel, desperate in a way only he could get, tears and snot making his face look raked with claws. "Damn. Fuck. *Roar*," he'd yelled at her. Then he'd run in his socks across the snowy yard. "Oh, no you don't!" Jill told him, as he fist-climbed an old ladder by the shed and crawled across the icy roof. She stood shivering in the doorway, her breath a dragony puff of smoke. She should go after him, she knew. She should follow him up the creaking ladder and somehow drag him back down. If she got him to his room, he'd tire himself eventually— he always did—but it seemed impossible right then to move across the threshold.

It was midwinter, had been winter for many months. Every night, the same.

Before he threw himself from the shed, he threw his Tonka truck. A drift of snow swallowed first one, then the other. They made no sound at all, which was interesting and oddly pleasant, as if she'd been let off the hook, granted reprieve for a crime she hadn't known she'd committed until it was over. She watched the spot where he'd fallen with singular intensity, seeing nothing but the broken drift until, gradually, each of the other parts of the night came back to her. The shed with their garage-sale bikes, the sagging house with its yellow lights, the snow so soundlessly dropping.

Mine, mine, mine, she thought.

Backyard swing, stop sign at the corner of Washington and Pine, the whole silent neighborhood.

Then her brother emerged from the snowdrift, wailing. She went to him. She went to him in her socks. His little body was slippery and hot, despite the dusting of snow and ice that covered him.

She kneeled down and pulled his wet head to her chest. "Shhh,"
she said to him. "Look, look." He was having trouble breathing.
He was gasping and couldn't get enough air to sob. "You jumped
off the shed and landed someplace else. I'm not really your sister.
That's not really your house. It looks similar, but it's not the same
place. You escaped! The Wizard came and took you away. Relax,
relax. You're not even *here*. It's okay."

*

When they get home from the Thai restaurant, Jill says something
disparaging about Manny's husband, but not because she doesn't
like him. In fact, she'd found him funny and smart, effortlessly
bearded. She's just feeling surly, every thought grinding itself
down to smaller, grittier thoughts.

"But they seem pretty happy!" Jill's boyfriend says, as he arranges
their leftovers in the refrigerator.

His beard is patchy. He's been learning German, and has words
on index cards taped to all their furniture. He touches the one on
the kitchen faucet, like a talisman, before filling a glass with *das
Wasser* and drinking.

"But predictable, you have to admit that."

"You had a nice time, I saw you." He sets his glass of water
down. "Come on. What makes you so committed to turning everything around so you're unhappy?"

Good question. Jill squints at him, preparing for another fight.
The problem with living with someone is that your every act can
be transformed into another example of their larger theory of you.
In fact, Jill has her own theories to slot him into—points about his
absent missionary father, his need for domestic reassurance—but
the feeling of a fight redounds before it starts, turns back on itself.

She walks forward and butts his ribcage with her head, ram-like.

He says, "Whoa, there," and rights her head, setting it against
his chest.

Her love for him has always been the underdog. She roots for
it as if from a distance. She imagines what they must look like

through the uncurtained window, the picture of tranquil domesticity they must now make. He smells like cilantro and beer, like curry and rain. And underneath that, he smells like himself, like nobody else, his body alarming because it is already so familiar.

*

Just before she's about to climb into bed, her mother calls again. She sounds like she's chewing something—a piece of gum? A fingernail? "I'm tired," she complains.

Jill nods, lifts the long tendril of a spider plant like the tail of a rat. Regretfully.

"My horoscope, listen. 'Mercantile energy makes love into an exchange.' It's true! He's twenty-eight, isn't he? Why can't he drive himself from here to there? Why can't he get to a store and buy his own food? Jill—"

Jill hangs up the phone. Just like that. Then she calls her mother back. She does this very calmly, making sure she hears a dial hum before she presses out the numbers. She takes a new tone this time. But of course it's an old tone, too—wasn't she always reprimanding her mother? Wasn't she always, as a teenager, lecturing her when Ryan got in trouble again at school?

"You know it doesn't work like that. Be reasonable. You can't just be done parenting when you choose."

"Oh, that's good, coming from you." Her mother chews and chews. Jill can hear her molars grinding, the sluice of her saliva around something soft. A caramel, a phone cord. "One day, you say, Poof. I wipe my hands of all this! I got other things to do! In a state three days away."

Jill draws a breath across the miles. "I'm not his mom."

*

But she was, in a way. She knew the trick. Whenever he threw a tantrum, whenever he started crying and couldn't stop, she just said, *You're not even here*, and he'd quiet down. He'd hang on her every word, fix her with his wet, red eyes. *The Wizard, remember, has taken you away.* You can't see or hear Him most of the time, but He

leaves signs to remind you. Everything is a sign. This Christmas
tree, and that clock, see how strange they are, almost glowing?
See how the squirrels just stand there and stare at you? See how
mysterious that snowman is? See that scary shadow the mailbox
casts, that cloud descending, isn't the weather off? Listen to how
funny I sound—doesn't my voice sound funny to you? You should
be careful. You left the old world behind and now there's another
one for you. You should try to get used to your new world.

*

She's in bed, almost asleep, when her boyfriend touches her.

He says, "My toenails feel soft. Are your toenails soft? We've
been sitting in wet shoes all night."

She draws up her knees and checks. She finds her toenails are
tough as teeth. We're not the same person, she wants to tell him.

He curls her hand in his, tries another tack. "How was volunteering today? I heard you say at dinner he was quite the terror."

She takes her hand back. "He's not so bad."

"That's probably your influence."

She purses her lips though she knows he's being nice. He believes in lulling each other to sleep with compliments. He wants
to wake up in each other's arms, plan a trip to Germany, send their
children to Montessori schools. He wants a future that comes as
painlessly as possible.

He says, sleepily, "Kids like that, they just need good role
models."

"I may not go back there," Jill tells him now, dragging her two
arms under her body for warmth. Lying on them. "I probably
won't."

*

Near the end of the session, Angelo had asked her from under the
table if maybe they could do math. He'd wanted to do *ten* times
things. Ten times two TVs. Ten times four microwaves. Jill thought
she understood why he wanted to play this game, so she'd put her
elbows on her skirted knees and pushed her eyebrows up.

"Did you have to live on the street for a while, honey?" She'd frowned, happy to have stumbled on this chance to flex her pity. "Did you lose all your stuff, your TV and your microwave?"

Angelo hadn't responded to that. Instead, he'd crawled farther under the table, across the room and into a box of donated clothes, where he buried himself in scarves and jackets.

She'd sat silently in the little classroom, feeling ridiculous. It would have been humiliating if one of the other volunteers had come in and found her like that, crouching in a plastic child's chair, alone, Angelo completely out of sight. But it would have been even more awkward to admit to the staff that her charge was hiding from her. So she just sat there, bleakly, reading on and on about cars and trucks and things that *go*. As she read, she saw out of the corner of her eye the toy airplane sitting on the math book, now dry. That's when she'd felt an impulse to put it in her own mouth. She'd wanted to shut herself up, show Angelo that she understood everything. If she hadn't been afraid of someone coming in—a teacher, another volunteer—she'd have put that plane in her mouth like a bit, like some horrible, punishing snack, and then she'd have crawled across the floor and into that box of clothes after him.

She'd wanted to do that! But the box of clothes across the room stood unmoving, and she'd had the strong impression she was all by herself. Wind plucked the green out of the trees through the window. The toy airplane windows looked up strangely at her, like black squirrel eyes. She blinked hard, twice. *You're not even here*, she thought.

*

After her brother is convicted and sentenced, he calls again. This time they don't talk much about weather. She can imagine what February in the northern Midwest is like without asking, and the truth is, it doesn't rain very often in Hollywood. They interrupt each other and pause. They're always awkward without a season in common. After a while, her brother talks a little about his car, the one that was impounded, and then he starts describing his drive home the night he was picked up by the cops.

"So you get off the 4 at Washington. Then you know how Washington curves?"

She knows those curves in her sleep. That was her world, those were her streets—she can feel how badly he wants to get back.

"Imagine doing those curves and getting to the top of the hill, and now you're right next to the high school, and it's downhill from there. You can see it. The house. You'll be there in a minute. Less. You're almost home in bed already. You could almost just go to sleep and wake up in the morning, you're that close. You're almost safe. The light is on. It's *right there.*"

In a flash she sees it all. The tall maples freighted with snow, Manny's old house down the road, her own stucco bungalow. She sees icicles hanging from every window, a light coming from her old bedroom, the old Magnavox throwing blue shadows across the yard.

"Did they catch you at the corner stop sign, then?" She's trying to capture the whole scene, trying to get back home again if she can, straining to see everything.

Her brother pauses, though, confused. "What do you mean? Where?"

"The one at Washington and Pine."

She hears his frustrated sigh. She hears him get bored, turn on the TV. "Jilly Bean. Jill. What the fuck? That stop sign's been gone for years."

LAKE ARCTURUS LODGE

It wasn't my husband that wanted the bear, it was me. Erich has always been so generous, so optimistic about people. When we opened for business, the lodge was empty as a lost castle, but he just said, "People will come when they do." He talked like this sometimes, which is one of the reasons I fell in love with him. He sounded like he'd given the world and its problems a good once-over and made up his mind without regrets. I admired his peace, because I was always getting trapped in thinking one way about a thing and then thinking the exact opposite. For instance, when we came up in '23 to these forsaken woods, I felt punished first, then blessed. The snow, especially, was a blankness I craved, not a blotting out, but a nursery for us. That first winter here we were born. I can't tell you how beautiful it was. We saw trees grow woolly as beasts with snow. We saw a moose with a beard of ice drop through the lake's crust and disappear altogether.

Funny, I don't remember exactly what Erich looked like then—though that was only a few years back, no time at all. I can remember what I did to him, but not what I saw. I held the teakettle with a damp cloth when I filled his cup. Sometimes, I broke ice from his moustache so he could talk, tiny corkscrews like claws, which melted in my fingers. He already had a moustache, though he was barely twenty years old, and now I remember what struck me then: his eyes were two different sizes. I used to wonder if he held one eye open wider than the other, if it was a matter of muscle rather than structure. I still don't know. My husband was good at everything else, so what did I care if he wasn't good-looking? He'd learned English in two years flat, the way other people learn cards or knitting. You could hear his determination in the way he talked, how poised he was in everything. From the beginning he spoke in a way that made me ashamed to have spoken English all my life. He was elegant as a diplomat, but more sincere.

Of course, he has always been good with his hands as well. He built this place with a crew of three in just two summers. During that time, I stayed in Duluth and scrounged up nice linens. Also carpets, couches, drapes. The third summer he put on a blue suit and I put on silk stockings and a hat, and we sat down to wait for guests in the lobby. I remember how miserably we chatted through those hours, our legs neatly crossed, our fingernails white. We had never courted properly (we met as teenagers, ate chicken, got married), but those first days at the lodge had all the ceremony and panic of a long date. Was there no future at all, we wondered. No guests or children to verify our efforts at contentment? We said many foolish things in our wish to escape such awkward circumstances. We talked of Chiang Kai-shek, of butterfly migrations, of stew.

"There's something in your hair," I told him one lonely afternoon.

He lifted his hand cautiously.

"Here," I said, rising. But I was lying, and he was already at the mirror in the hallway, turning his head. I remember his bow tie was crooked and looked something like a badly plucked flower. I couldn't help smiling at him. Even then, I was always getting kindness and cruelty confused, so I can't be exactly sure why his dishevelment made me so happy.

We had to coax our first guests to us. The locals were suspicious. You know how logging people are, so territorial and shifty. They couldn't understand why we made such a show of everything, why we carted in candelabras and pickles. I admit we didn't know why we did these things either. After Mamma's inheritance was gone, we spent a great deal of time washing things down, fluffing pillows, pressing napkins. We made an earnest effort to be as grand as possible. Can you imagine? We had ideas about hotels from Davenport and Redwing; we expected weekenders, not hunters and fishermen. But who rides the train to Duluth, then takes a steamer to Marais or a float plane to Ely for the *weekend*? The lodge had five big rooms upstairs and two small rooms off the lobby. The longer the place sat empty the harder we tried, until everything started seeming like an instance of decoration. In those first days, I floated lupine petals in the water basins, arranged butterscotches in bowls. I knew tea roses would die, but I planted them anyway, in a daze of hopeless opulence and inevitable waste.

We didn't know the first thing about lake country. I grew up on cobbled streets, with sidewalks and gas lamps; my husband had escaped as a teenager from a nail factory in Bremen. I admit I thought of our lake primarily as transportation to town and scenery through our windows. I was bewildered to see Erich so charmed by it. I remember watching him sink an arm into the depths, splash up a bit of water into his mouth, flick his face dry. He took the boat out at night and rowed to the logging camp on the far side of the lake, where the rocks were as wide as automobiles. He learned to trap from the logging people there, who kept him some nights. He learned to bring down a pine without fuss and float it across the waves, slim ship bound for furniture.

The lake yielded up our tables and chairs in this way, and other
surprises too. The summer we opened we found a floating broom, a
fox pup under our canoe, and Leif Williams. Leif was our first real
guest, and he just capsized his boat during a storm, so we didn't
charge him anything. We were nervous as new mothers around
him. During the night, we argued over whether we should leave a
lantern burning in the hallway, whether we should wake him for
breakfast or let him sleep. Leif was a good sport, a middle-aged
fisherman with a cabin out west, and we convinced him to stay
a few nights after the storm dissipated into occasional columns
of rain. With his pale blue eyes and black eyebrows, Leif had a
shambling, uneasy, angelic look about him. He said his mother had
died in an avalanche in the Rocky Mountains. After a few glasses
of Canadian gin, he confessed he'd clawed his way out of the snow
and left her buried beneath him. He kept saying, "I just wanted to
survive, but now I can't do nothing. I'm a napkin. I'm rust."

We kept him for three nights. We gave him pies and towels, a
boat ride to the falls, a kite. By the time he left, we were disconso-
late and proud. We felt as if the very best of ourselves was paddling
off toward Canada, the only useful thing we'd ever done.

Goldie came next, and she only came because I asked her. I sent
her a simple but pleading letter, and she arrived at the logging
camp across the lake with two trunks, a kitten in a cage, and a
hammock from Mexico. The hammock was a gift for our porch.
Goldie was my second cousin, tall and frizzy-haired, unmarried.
The first thing she said to us was: "I'm so, so sorry!" She gripped my
arm, almost painfully, explaining she was late, she was unkempt,
she was tired. I told her "Nonsense!" but in truth her apologies
were charming, inventive, almost intimate, like confessions. When
I told her to stop apologizing, she apologized—warmly, enthusiastically—for that.

She settled into one of the rooms on the second floor, shyly,
hanging her frocks on the bedpost, and stayed for a long time.
When her kitten left stools like crusty larva behind the drapes,

Erich swept them discreetly into a basket. I never told him that I asked her to come.

My husband wanted babies and I gave him guests instead. Should I be ashamed? By the time the lodge opened, we'd been together five years. I was the only married woman I knew without children. We didn't sleep well at night—there were mosquitoes, heat waves, other lonelinesses—but it wasn't that we didn't try. I should revise that a bit. I had nightmares in which I was sick, blistering with tumors, malignant as death: I was pregnant in every one. I woke up with my hands on my breasts, arms crossed, my own fingers harassing my nipples like mouths. In my dreams, I lived in a pit of children. Their hands were the same size and texture as their gums, as their earlobes and faces. Everything could gnaw in a hideous, painless way without teeth.

I won't pretend I wasn't chastened and relieved to wake up empty, myself. I really thought I might be able to avoid that kind of grave forever, if I tried. Erich grew melancholy after a time, but I grew industrious. After the first week, I boiled Goldie's sheets and ours in an iron pot over the fire out back. I stayed up late one night and baked a slippery yellow cake with canned pineapple.

"Her name is Sugar," Goldie said of the kitten, around that time. That was a night when we were feeding Goldie pike caught two lakes over, the gin Leif left us, and imported jelly. The kitten was on her lap, humming unremittingly. Goldie made a face, then put her hand on my husband's arm when he stooped to retrieve her plate. "Isn't that terrible? Isn't that just the first thing you'd think of?"

I saw him sit down and put his head in his hand, as if thinking the matter over very seriously. Since Goldie had arrived, I'd seen something new in him, a tolerance and almost gift for inanity. It was like hearing him speak in German, seeing this ease with something so alien to me. I knew him only as hard-minded and grave. With her, he lifted his eyebrows. He grinned in a way that parted his moustache.

"Will the cat understand his name? Or is this name for you?"

"It's how I feel about him, I guess." She took a curl from her head and placed it absent-mindedly in her ear. "He's stupid, of course. He won't know Bob from Pumpkin."

"Stupid's a good name."

"Stupid?" Goldie asked. She lifted the cat up under the armpits and stuck out her tongue at it.

Erich was beaming. I was impressed by his ease with her and, at the same time, irritated. He grew up in a German factory town, worked like a dog to stay alive during the war, snuck away on a boat when he was sixteen. He always seemed to me like a wizened old man under his young skin, his soul worn to the point of sere-nity. Who was I to forbid him whimsy?

Later that week, I told Goldie my husband needed help in the garden, and out she went, apologizing as she left for not helping sooner. I was half in love with Goldie myself for years, so I knew what it meant to be around her. She was five years younger than me and so thin she was always bent forward or backward at the waist, as if unable to fully support the upper half of her body. She believed she was ugly, which made her lovelier than she was. Even I liked to watch her in humid weather, pulling hair from her ear in a perfect coil, like the tendril of a newborn plant. She was super-ficial, an oddball with nice teeth, but we couldn't get enough of her. We gave her meals we couldn't afford, grew severe and nasty to each other in our guilt over the waste, came from our quarrels clean, as if they were a form of hygiene.

Goldie stayed so long, we went through all the pickles and scented soap in the pantry. With these amenities gone, we spent days on the dock, shoeless, Goldie and I playing cards, Erich reading about fishing lures in out-of-date magazines. It felt a little like I imagi-ned university might feel if we'd gone, all that indolence and talk, all that lazy thinking. In July, we watched a hornet hive form high in a tree, bulbous and sound as a football. In August, the lake started to smell and dry up a little, leaving strangely punctured fish on the shoreline. When the muskrats came for the fish, I started to worry that Goldie had misunderstood my invitation. She had been with us for almost five weeks; she was kind, but not rich, and Erich knew it.

One morning around that time, he woke up and put on old trousers instead of his suit. I could only guess he'd picked up part-time work across the lake, chasing or climbing, whatever grunt jobs they gave foreigners. I watched him work a soft leather belt through the loops. He was just about to leave the room when I bolted up and yelled, "Wait!" He turned around.

"Why don't we talk?"

"Sure," he said.

"We don't have to have everything worked out," I told him. But you know how people say things to convince themselves, how every word is part lie because it crosses out and denies one quadrant of truth. Of course everything had to work out.

"It *won't*," he assured me, coming back, putting his hand on my forehead. Reassured as I felt, I disliked how he needed so little from me.

I started to cry. One half of my body was under sheets. The other half, like a figure on the prow of a ship, arched mutantly toward him. What was wrong with me? I kissed him, resentfully. I held my lips over my teeth and bit him until he came back for me. I wanted him to wear trousers—he was a clown in his suit, an imbecile—but I didn't want him to want to. We were far too young to stop pretending.

Later that day, I went into town and telephoned Grace Wilson, an old Saint Paul acquaintance who I knew from rumors had married well. I made her agree to come to the lodge by reminding her that she owed me. In high school, I'd covered for her when she accepted marriage proposals from two boys at once and needed an excuse for one when she saw the other. It was a sacrifice of my dignity to do this, but Goldie wasn't going to pay our bills, and we had hornets in the pantry. My mother's good silver was tarnishing, and I couldn't bring myself to polish anymore what no one used.

The Wilsons flew in from Duluth on a chartered float plane. The plane sent waves knocking against the shore, drenching the steely rocks, overturning Erich's cedar-rib canoe. When Grace stepped out onto our dock, I saw she was wearing white gloves and a funny type of moccasin. She held out a booted foot and said, "Look what I bought in Duluth! Indian shoes. What do you call them, Harold?" She touched my sleeve. "Good for *creeping.*"

She took a few tiptoeing warrior steps across the wet planks.

Two nondescript boys in raincoats lumbered onto shore and commenced digging a hole beneath some pines. Harold, not one of the fiancés from high school, surveyed the lake, stepped gingerly over an invisible hazard on the rocks, and made his way toward the woods. Erich called after him, "Can I take your bag?"

The man turned, sulkily, imperious, and then a shift went over his face, as if he'd found an old friend in a crowd of strangers, and he said, "I don't believe in packing much, thank you. Look here, I have all I need in this hamper." He opened one hinged lid and pointed out the contents, obviously delighted by his own thrift.

Grace put her arm in mine and whispered, "Harold's writing a book, but he hasn't actually written anything yet because he's rich. Would you believe it, Midge?" She affected a pained expression. Behind her, the chartered plane gutted the lake and lifted over far trees. "I'm *moneyed* people."

For the first time that summer, the lodge was nearly full. We put the boys in one room and their governess, a tanned woman with a Texan accent, in the room next door. We gave Grace and Harold the room over the porch, with a view of the lake at sunset. Unlike Goldie, the Wilsons were loud and busy guests, inexhaustible. The boys brought turtles to the bathtub, pebbles to the dinner table, an antler to bed. They had an idea about the physics of air and were determined to build a craft that could float them over the lake like a balloon. I talked with them about this at length and could never determine the extent to which they knew they were playing. Jasper was six, and he became furious with his little brother, Jake, at any suggestion that the venture was not possible. On the shore there were complicated arrangements of thistle and jars. For days, they claimed their failure was due to sabotage by locals: sometimes Indians, sometimes wolves. Then one morning they came to the dining room before breakfast almost sobbing, saying they had done it, they made it to the other side.

"Why are you crying, then?" their mother pointed out. She was mocking them because all of us were watching, and I think Grace knew she was better at winning a crowd than raising children. Jasper reddened at his mother's words, clearly crushed. He explained, putting his face into his armpit and taking it out again, "Jake's crying because he's a *baby!*" Grace turned to scold the governess for negligence, but the boys were sopping wet, breathless, and I believed they believed that they had done what they said.

I told them this. That night I went to their bedroom and touched their heads. I said, "Good job, boys!" but they looked at me in a sickened way, barely tolerating my presence. I realized I'd made a mistake, but I had trouble sorting out what it was exactly.

I won't say we became friends with Harold and Grace, but something else happened that was a little more complicated. A week after they arrived, I ran into Harold smoking a pipe and he asked me to help him out of his marriage. He was sitting in the woods under a line of laundry I was drying, and he spoke simply, his mouth around the neck of the pipe. His words sounded lazy and offhand, almost unintentional. Then he took the pipe from his lips and put the warm mouthpiece against my ankle.

That night, I lay with my husband in our bed and gently stroked his throat. He liked that, and it frightened me a little how vulnerable he was with his chin thrust up—how bony and ridged it was there, like the spine of a small, extinct reptile. "We should think of

ways to draw more people here," I told him, fingering the hump
of his Adam's apple. "We should advertise in the paper. We should
make signs for the road."

He said for the second time, "People will come when they do."

"But what for?" I felt a lurch of desperation. It was as if he refused to understand the basic machinery involved in being human,
how one thing led to the next. He had a fixed notion that all lives
were as pure as his own, born of unqualified, disciplined intentions.

In the next weeks, I took pains to avoid face-to-face conversations
with Harold and Grace. They were spoiled and self-involved, and
though I didn't approve of them at all, I found I enjoyed watching
them from a distance. I grew interested in their diets, for instance:
in Harold's taste for slightly soured milk and the way Grace picked
at her fish. She slid her fork between the bones as if performing
surgery, totally absorbed, frightened whenever she took a bite. I
kept serving fish so I could watch her at this task, which made
her seem vulnerable like nothing else, strangely animal and vital. I
grew fascinated by the way Harold and Grace derided each other,
rarely speaking to each other in public, but always lightly narrat-
ing the other's faults for audiences. They seemed pleased rather
than discomfited by the disorders they pointed out, announcing
them like accomplishments: "Grace thinks books are for propping
open windows," or "Harold, bless his heart, never learned to leave
his mosquito bites alone. Look! He's like someone with pox." I
liked best to hear them in their room at night, shouting. "You're
unnecessary to my happiness," I once heard Grace say, and though
I didn't hear the context, the phrase struck me as so ruthless, so
wonderful, it ran through my head whenever Erich's disappointment in me showed. I imagined him saying it to me, the clean
shard I'd become when he hissed in my face, *You're unnecessary to
my happiness.* Of course, my husband was tender and formal most
of the time. After the Wilsons came, he wore his suit every day
again, like a man at an everlasting funeral. At night, he almost

begged me to get pregnant; touching each other was like sitting in the empty lodge waiting for guests who never arrived; we were humiliated to find the other always present for our personal failures.

He kept saying, like a man purchasing milk, "Thank you!"

"Don't say that," I told him, annoyed because I didn't want to be held accountable. I wanted his anger or forgiveness, but not his false gratitude for this: the baby my body refused to bear.

Once, the Wilsons wanted a picnic excursion, and when I went out to untie the canoes, I saw something beneath the dock. Not a broom or a fox pup, but Leif's kite, the one Erich and I gave him. It was caught beneath the planks like a sea animal, a thing from school books, not from lakes: yellow, red, and green. I got down on my knees to fish it out. For just a moment with my hands in the water, I believed that Leif was down there with it, floating white beard and blind newt hands, but then there was a gulping sound and water streamed down my arms. The kite was a wet heap in my hands.

"What you got there?" Erich called from the bank.

What could I say about this? I suppose we could have laughed together—what had we been *thinking*, giving a grown man a kite?—but I still felt something of Leif in my arms, which was disconcerting, unbearable in fact, so I lowered the thing back into the water. I didn't want Erich to see it, to worry about what had happened to our first brief guest.

"Nothing," I said. "Just a shirt, someone's lost laundry."

He called, "Bring it up, we'll dry it off," because my husband had industry enough to cast on any object at hand, wayward guest or washed-up trash, any irrecoverable article.

But I said, scolding, guilty: "No, it's ruined."

I went to him myself. I climbed the rocky bank and smoothed his moustache with a finger still wet with lake water. He lifted his eyebrows but did not move his face an inch, his breath coming through his slightly parted lips, like the minute, barely discernible current through two logs in the lodge. Gently, I put my mouth over that fragile draft, kissed him. His lips were papery, desiccated against my own.

Was it then that possibilities began to dawn on me that hadn't before? I'd been so certain for so long that it was some failure in me that kept Erich from the family he wanted. That it was me, and not him.

Of course that day's suspicions were only confirmed much later, long after the Wilsons left. So it's possible I'm rearranging the order of my feelings now to justify what I did to him.

The circus in Duluth was Grace's idea. Somehow she got us all to go with her. It was a long trip—six hours in a hired car on logging roads, then another lengthy stretch on the Superior steamer—and I'd grown restless, I suppose, weary of the barren lake, the immaculate order of pines. I craved some adventure and disorder. Goldie wore her hair in yellow ribbons, and the boys put on shoes again for the first time in a week. Even Erich went along, though he got carsick on the drive and had to sit with his head hanging out the window like someone's forlorn dog. We all stayed two nights in a ramshackle Victorian hotel in a residential neighborhood. The place had running water and electric lights, but Erich and I could not help but feel a vague competitive dislike for the rumpled maid and diminutive doorman. I'm not proud to say we colluded in disparaging the place whenever the Wilsons were around, affecting a businesslike scorn at every attempt at convenience. We took pleasure in pointing at a crusty orange formation beneath the porch and making Grace put her hand to her breast. "Yuck," I lamented. "What on earth could that be?"

The circus was a few miles out of town at the county fairgrounds. We sat together on bleachers under the sun, balancing our hats on our heads and squinting like people who'd lived for a long time underground. I couldn't tell if all that squinting and sweating behind the ears made me feel oppressed or ebullient.

I remember Goldie spent the day with the boys, shunning the governess who was reading a newspaper and eating a snow cone. Grace and Harold settled in next to each other on the bench, argued for a moment about whether the seats were any good, and didn't speak to each other for the rest of the show. Erich and I sat on either side of them.

If you've been to a circus, you know how they manage to make preposterous things seem ordinary, even dispiriting. We saw three midget children riding hounds, for instance. The children had shiny leather saddles and clown noses, and though everyone clapped, I kept expecting something more thrilling to happen. It was like a trail ride, the way those big-boned dogs lumbered their figure eights, the way the midget boys gripped their tiny pommels. Then a portly man in a wedding dress rummaged in his sleeve for a crumpled bouquet of daisies. After dancing about on his toes, he plucked the bouquet, petal by browning petal, and ate it. I felt like I was watching something I'd done myself—though in private, abashed—and I admired his shameless regurgitation. The bouquet came out of his mouth whole, reconstituted, wet. When he bowed and gave it to a woman in the audience, she held it far away from her body with two fat fingers.

Beside me, Harold offered up a piece of popcorn. I set the foamy, tasteless thing on my tongue and let it dissolve to its kernel. He positioned his knee so it lined up with mine.

"That's disgusting," I told him, stoutly, pointing out two scantily clad obese women doing the polka. But it wasn't at all. It wasn't disgusting or even strange, just one of the ways the universe worked. If you were very fat and a twin, you learned at a young age to dance for audiences.

During intermission, Goldie took the boys to look at the horses, and the governess stayed absorbed in her newspaper comics. The rest of us wandered over to the auction set up beneath a canopy across a dusty field. Circling in silence the tables of linens and bicycles, I had a curious, nervous feeling, as if we were waiting for something to happen: as if we'd all set our marbles rolling down a ramp and we were now just watching to see how they'd collide. Grace and my husband were discussing the merits of putting a bid down for a painted wicker throne, which Grace thought would look good on the porch of the lodge. They were almost bickering over it, actually, the way Grace bickered with Harold, and I was about to join in when a man in suspenders distracted me. "What's this?" he kept saying, a little too loudly. I followed his gaze until we were both looking into a cage of sorts, but what was inside perplexed me for a moment. I wanted to say, *Bear*, but it wasn't exactly. It was a couch, an old man, a wilderness. It was the first thing that had really surprised me in a long time, and before I even realized it was dead, I knew I could use it.

"Is that thing *for sale?*" the man asked.

Harold took my elbow and tugged it. "Do you want to take a walk outside?" He was not suave so much as needling. I looked at him impatiently and saw his hair was greasy. It was flat as a swimming cap over his eyebrows.

He started talking about his book. It was to be an exploration of the rift between loggers and conservationists, he said, a lesson on, no, a love letter *to* the wilderness. This was a new idea, something he'd discovered while sitting on a rock in our woods, and he'd already come up with many good metaphors for pine needles. *Rodeo tassels*, he said, shyly now, as if offering me a choice delicacy from his plate. *The fringe of a lady's dress.* For goodness' sake. Why was there no machine to lift boys over water, never any real artists, but always some fop of a husband dreaming his commonplace dreams of adultery? Rodeo tassels could not interest me, could interest no one.

I looked him square in the eye and said, "You're unnecessary to my happiness." I meant it to be kind, honestly. I meant it to release him from whatever responsibility he felt to impress me.

But it was only after I had said it—and felt its correct and appropriate violence—that I realized that the comment was neither original nor true. Of course, I needed him. It was childish to think otherwise. I needed his money before the end of the month; I needed him to tell his wealthy friends about the lodge and its comforts; I needed his wife to cheer my husband when I could not. I looked over at them assessing the wicker throne, Grace sitting in it like the queen she was, Erich rolling his eyes like a man who knew exactly what she was and was not bothered by it.

I pulled a strand of hair from Harold's shirt, apologetic now for what I'd said. I knew how to flirt as well as anyone. I said of the strand of hair, holding it up and leaning in: "Hers or mine?"

He was relieved and smiled, almost winningly. It was then that I let him grope for and take my hand. Of course, I didn't outline any plan for him, nor promise right then to be his mistress, but you how the human mind works. I did a quick calculation: there were still three and a half weeks of summer and two unused beds in the lodge. And what is logic, after all, but the way the mind takes control of facts and arranges them to suit its own interests? I wanted some measure of control over my husband's and my circumstances. I wanted that most of all. And Harold? He wanted to be flattered.

We got the bear carcass for almost nothing. I thought we should stuff it right there in Duluth, as the thing had been dead a full day already, but Erich said he knew a good taxidermist outside Grand Marais. We found an empty logging truck that was going up north that afternoon and paid six dollars for the bear to go with it. It took three men to sling the thing onto the pallet, wearing leather gloves and cloths around their noses. Flies were already distorting its face, nursing its rear end. Grace was horrified, but the boys were ecstatic, absolutely jittery with love for the thing. Both these reactions pleased me very much. Before it drove off, the boys kept skipping around the truck, stroking the bear with sticks and touching its clipped, opal claws.

I could not stop talking at dinner that night, working out the details of my idea for the bear's new life as a feature in our lobby.

I thought we could hire a photographer to take a picture of it, put ads in papers in Minneapolis and Chicago, draw rich, outdoorsy people with the spectacle their unexceptional imaginations desired. I drank a lot of coffee, and found my hands were shaking when I lifted my mug, as if my body had been starved and was finally being fed again. Everything was so pleasant and unnerving. I wanted Erich to feel this as well, wanted him to see how things were going to work out for us now, but he was too worried about how much dinner would cost. I saw him peering at the bill over his spectacles, ever innocent. Very tenderly, I corrected his math.

Our guests last summer were our children, I raised every one of them myself: Leif Williams, Goldie, the Wilsons. By fall, we had other types of people, drunk fishermen who were standoffish and strangers to me, but the summer guests were mine. On the last leg of our journey home from Duluth, paddling across the lake, we sang impolite logging songs the boys had picked up over their weeks in our woods. *Fellows at the grand ole gates, say hello to your bosomed fates!* We pitched in our canoes, but I don't think I was alone that day in feeling vouchsafed against danger. Even the moose in our garden was hard to take seriously. We stood with our bags on the dock, a little uneasy, yes, but then Jasper and Jake went up so close they could have touched its black muzzle. They raised sticks to prod its hindquarters.

"Stay back," Erich warned them, but the moose was docile as a donkey, knock-kneed, a circus pet. For an instant, I confused him with the bear we bought and felt sorry. His obdurate gentleness made my heart sink, because I knew there was something sick in him we couldn't see, a malignancy that softened and destroyed his nature. A murky layer of film wobbled over each eye. He walked in a nice circle, very showy and staged, and then everybody clapped when he took a step back and shambled into the woods. My pounding heart grew too loud, and I had to put my hands on my knees, prevent a spinning sensation from pulling me down, and then pretend it didn't happen, pretend I was fine, and the moose was just another entertainment, and the bear—a thing that walked on a leash and balanced a ball—was once a vicious beast. And who was to say they were not.

All winter Erich has been splitting wood till dusk. Nights, he holds onto my strange, new body out of practical necessity, for warmth, teeth chattering in my ear. I can feel his worry going through me in shudders. But under that worry I can sense how pleased he is. He must be happy in his way, grateful to have the future coming so smoothly now, or else why does he fall asleep before I do, giving me up to the cold, forgetting everything?

I feel I just need to get to spring. In a few more weeks, the ice will be pulling away from the shore and mallards will be returning. Guests will be coming back for walleye. The doctor has promised I'll be back to my old self by then, but he's country people and doesn't even bother to shave properly. Whenever he bends over me, I can see the stubble on his face like dirt. I haven't told that stubble-faced doctor that I barely feel any kicks. I think I understand the baby's silence. I've prepared my own silence for her, after all. She'll have her life and her father, her future with its fine logic, ah, maybe even my good skin, my small, dark eyes. But her secrets, those are *mine*. I'll carry them for her and I won't mind. I'm proud of them.

HERE, STILL

I do not like her much, Lora, my best friend. She is freckled daintily on her arms and chest, and wears low-cut blouses so you can see the bones of her clavicles. She has never been ashamed of her little breasts. She once held me under water, her hands on my head, and when I shoved her off, gasping, she kissed me. Her hair was long and wet, and it draped like a cape over her shoulders.

"There, Amanda," she said. Lora's smile was ferocious: her lips thin, her teeth barely showing. "Now don't you feel better?" I held my fingers to the burn in my nose, and she waded back to the shore. The bow that held her bikini was a pair of turquoise wings.

That was when we were sixteen. Since then, we've established the terms of our friendship over the phone, long conversations intensified by infrequency. Once, we didn't speak for more than a year, and Lora left occasional caustic messages on my voicemail: "Are you busy or dead?" When I finally called her back, she wouldn't speak after hello.

"Lora." I remember pressing the phone into my head. I could feel my ear squished up, like a mollusk, inside the receiver. "I know you're there. Please say something back."

She grumbled a few words, quietly at first, so I had to ask her to repeat herself.

"What? What?"

"I said *something back*."

I cleared my throat. I imagined her across all those miles, Lora, with her lavish red nails, fingering the dry skin on her elbows.

This is how you keep a best friend: you talk out of guilt, you live in separate states. Again and again, you vow fidelity to her in fits of absurd hopefulness. It is the same as being in love.

I finally went to visit her the summer I left Tom. She was living in her parents' house, a pretty rambler in an old part of town, shaded by pines like a forest cabin. No one had mown the lawn for weeks, since late spring perhaps, when her parents had moved one by one into the nursing home. Grass stalks bristled with seed in the flower gardens.

Inside the shades were pulled. The air was sweet, air freshener covering an odor with an edge, maybe urine. Lora took my bag and brushed my bangs back with her hand, as if checking for a fever.

"You should grow those out."

"Hello, Lora." I tried to give her a hug, but she was taller than I remembered. I settled for propping my chin on the bone of her shoulder. She was barefoot in a beige pantsuit.

"Don't look at me like that." She raised one manicured eyebrow. "Try working at Kohl's in fishnets."

It had been three years since I'd seen her last. In all that time I had never once pictured her face. It struck me now as symmetrical, but prematurely aged, as if she had smiled too extravagantly in her thirty-four years. Though she wasn't quite smiling now, I could see exactly how her face would crease if she were. Her freckles were beginning to merge into a brown smudge on her nose.

"Cookie?" She held out a box of Thin Mints. I took one, but the softened cookie made me feel vaguely obscene, and I held it without taking a bite.

I asked, "Didn't you get a dog?"

"Oh, him! There's this lady down the street who wooed him away with sausage links. He started visiting her when I was at work, and now he's taken to her bed. I prefer to think he's been run over by a truck."

"Do you miss him?" I was trying for pleasantness. In Lora's presence, pleasantries were a defeat.

"Not really. Men are better, and he was always making me choose. Nimrod didn't like human males over four feet tall."

She dropped onto the couch, putting her feet on the coffee table and closing her eyes. The cookie had melted a hat around my thumb, and I put the slippery lump in my mouth to be rid of it.

"And what about Tom?"

I didn't answer right away because I was busy arranging my body on the couch. I licked my fingers, uneasily. I told myself: don't be sick. Always, well-lived-in houses like this made me feel swallowed up, forced by inevitable processes through someone else's gut. There were fecal-looking statuettes on the mantel.

I decided to cross my legs. "Well. He took this new job downtown—"

"Who did he fall in love with?"

"No one!"

"Just say he's dead, like Nimrod. Run over on the street. It'll make you feel better."

"It's not like that." I propped a pillow behind my back. I put another on my lap and smoothed its fringe with my sticky fingers. I tried to focus on Tom, but I could only come up with a mental outline of him, his face cut out like one of those cardboard cowboys at the carnival. The thing was, I was happy with him for years. I remembered being happy as if it were a trick someone played, the universe setting me up on a blind date with good fortune. I thought of how Tom combed his hair before he came to bed, the way he once wore swimming goggles in a snowstorm. I made a list of his traits—long eyelashes, droopy earlobes—then grew tired of the task and stood up.

"He's dead."

"Really?" Lora said. "I never liked him much anyway."

"He's dead," I told her again, because it was so nice to say and so absolutely right. When had he ever been truly alive to me? Nearly every night for two years, we'd eaten dinner on a tiny mounted table that swung on a hinge from his kitchen wall. I left him not long after the hinge on the table broke, when I started to seriously worry that what I really wanted was the nightly routine of unlatching the top, lowering the wooden panel so I could set out two plates side by side.

It wasn't that Lora couldn't sleep, but she chose to avoid her dreams, which she said were better than life. "I don't need the disappointment in the morning," she told me, scooping coffee grounds into the paper filter. She poured us shots of whisky while we waited for our frozen pizza to cook and the coffee to percolate. Lora never changed her clothes after work, and late in the evenings she started to remind me of a tent: damp in the summer heat and wrinkling on the couch. She'd wave the remote control at the TV, making a fuss, her skirt a khaki twist around her hips. Sometimes she'd shed the skirt and ride the exercise bike in just her panty hose.

"Sleep, if you want," she told me when it got late. But it was an accusation.

We decided to learn Greek. I sat with her on the back deck in the dark, drinking tepid coffee with whisky from a flowered mug. The pines above us were so thick, so confused with branches and trunks, I couldn't see the stars.

"I feel dizzy," I read. "*Esthanomai zaladha.* I've been bitten by a snake." The phrasebook was from our trip to Europe some years back, when we slept on trains and saw most countries in the dark. It had been December then, the cities draped in Christmas lights, so every country looked the same. We had phrase books for French and Italian too.

"Did we ever speak Greek when we were there?" Lora had a hole in the toe of her pantyhose, and one yellowy nail poked through. She worked at the hole, making room for more toes.

"I remember *alithos anesti*. He is risen, indeed."

"Right, all those hunchbacked monks. There was that monastery with the goats, what was it called?"

I could not remember any goats. But I did recall the motherly monks, swooshing about in their death-black robes. One had given me a piece of Juicy Fruit for taking a picture of him with his hockey stick. I glanced at Lora and saw her grinning in the dark. I hoped I was smiling too, so we could be happy together.

After a while, Lora said, "I'm bored."

Carefully, I squeezed my thighs together. I considered commenting on the fireflies, which I'd been saving for a silence like this. All my life, I was saving fireflies for her, tidbits of conversation, or funny, witnessed scenes. Even when I hadn't spoken to her in months, I'd see a child licking his dog and think: Lora might close her eyes and laugh out loud.

To offset her growing restlessness, I pointed at the dark. "They're beetles!" I announced.

Lora had her face in her mug, sipping. "What?"

"Fireflies are. I think."

"Fireflies? I've heard the males choreograph their blinking and voila! The females go crazy." She sneered. "Look how they've mesmerized you, Manda. You're a beetle at heart."

She was right. I drew up my knees to my chest and let my body be round and hard. I tried to think of something else to say, something better, but before I could, Lora was standing and stretching. She was gathering up the open phrase books from the deck planks.

"God, this is so exhausting."

I took in a sharp breath—unduly wounded.

She added, "Isn't it exhausting getting drunk like this every night?"

I exhaled, slowly, keeping my eyes on the woods as if I couldn't bear to look away. Really, I was afraid of the look I might catch on Lora's face: her frank, inevitable disappointment.

Lora claimed she didn't dream with less than four hours of sleep. Though she'd idle away the night on the deck or in front of the TV, she finally went to bed in a great rush, barely pausing in the bathroom to pee. I'd be the one awake when the birds started up— caffeinated and woozy both—lying flat on my back on the living room couch. Birds in the dark are the dreariest things. Sometimes, irritated, I'd try to will my way to Lora's dreams, which I felt she had no right to, having given them up. At first I thought of them as books on a shelf, books piled up and untouched, but that seemed too academic, so I made them animals instead. Lora's dreams should be hairy and hoofed. I imagined scrambling past the monks, tracking the beasts across the rocks, across Greece, which I transformed into Six Flags with ruins. After that, I could not think what was better than life so I didn't dream any further. Probably I wasn't really dreaming anyway, because I could hear a dog barking down the street. I could hear Lora breathing loudly in her sleep, far beyond dreams.

When Tom called on Saturday, Lora was at the nursing home. I knew she had wanted me to go with her by the way she draped herself over furniture on her way out the door. She flopped on the couch in her sunglasses; she lay belly-down on the bureau to reach her keys. Lora knew how to make her body slow down so you'd pay attention to her.

"It smells, it smells!" She twisted up her face. "They have an old-people stink, like babies, but sweeter. They're too sweet, that's their problem." She stood in the doorway now, her face suddenly solemn. "If my mother asks me to powder her face, I'll refuse."

She lingered in her car, rolling down the passenger window so she could wave out at me. She looked like someone on her way across the world.

Back inside the house, I straightened the magazines and watered the dead plants. I kept at these domestic tasks because, after four days, I was still unnerved by so many used-up objects in one place: yellowing curtains, sticky countertops. There was a stain on the living room carpet where I could not bring myself to step. Sometimes when I was alone there, I was surprised at how little of Lora was left, and I half expected to come across her parents on the stairway. I'd never liked the Martins much—when we were girls and they played pinochle on the deck—but they did seem unaccountably durable.

I was cleaning out the Martins' ice trays when the telephone rang. "Amanda? Is that you?"

I knew it was unkind to laugh, but he sounded so painfully earnest, like Oliver Twist with his empty bowl.

I swallowed hard. "Hello."

"You said you might visit Lora, and your cell's been disconnected, and—" Tom tended to pour his sentences out. "—Mandie, how *are* you? How have you been since—"

"I'm fine. It's nice spending time with Lora."

He checked himself. "How is Lora doing?"

"Lora's herself." I thought of her as she was last night, clipping her toenails on the counter while I cut the broccoli. "She's not here," I said, gratuitously.

He told me how much he'd always liked Lora. She has an interesting face, he said, she reminded him of a president. He hoped we were enjoying ourselves. "Have fun!" he said, so cheerlessly that I knew the time had come for me to ask about him.

"Tom," I started. There must be some rule about being nice to harmless things. "Everything. Okay?"

"Well. Actually, things are—"

I didn't want to know. I resented his street-urchin voice, begging through the phone.

"—not so good. There's something I need to tell you."

I remembered then what I'd said about him when I first arrived at Lora's. *He's dead.* For an instant, it seemed like something I'd actually done to him: Tom had always been so literal and obedient. I wondered, fleetingly, if his end would come slowly or fast, whether he was, even now, pale and drawn as a queen from the eighteenth century. He seemed to be breathing strangely.

"Tom—" Guilt made me whiny. I tried again, now with a secretary's voice, efficient, I hoped, but kind. "Tom. I'm glad to hear from you, but now's not a good time to *get into things.* I hear Lora's car in the driveway, and she's been with her parents, who are, I don't know if you know, *dying.*" I winced as I said the word to him.

"Oh. I'm sorry." I could almost hear his fingers in his hair. "Does she know there are support groups for things like that? Does she have the legal issues figured out?"

My heart's a prune, I thought, and yours is a gigantic mouth.

"I've got to go, Tom."

"Right. Okay."

When Lora came in, she bounced her palm off the top of my head as she walked by. "So, there are you are."

"What do you mean?"

"My dad kept asking about you, so I told him you were just waiting out in the hall. He said, tell her to come in! But when I went to get you, lo and behold, you weren't there!"

My eyebrows felt damp. "Now he'll think I'm rude."

"Does it matter?"

She went out the back door to the deck and down the stairs. I followed her out, my socks on the wet wood making me cringe. At the bottom of the deck stairs I stopped, watching Lora wade into the grass.

"You know—" She didn't turn back. "—I never really saw my father in bed before all this. Is that weird? When I was little, it seemed like he never slept, and when he did, he did it behind closed doors." She was across the lawn now, almost to the woods.

I was hesitating on the bottom step; she was pulling something out of the grass. I couldn't see what it was at first, something covered in a plastic tarp. The tarp flashed as it came off, making me think of a magician's trick, a white scarf whisked back to reveal a red-eyed bird. "Fuck," Lora muttered, wiping at her shirt. She dragged the lawnmower with one hand across the grass.

"What are you doing?" I felt contemptible in my socks, as if a person needed shoes to be intelligent.

"Mowing." She never looked up. She paused to push back her hair.

"Why now?"

"Because my father wants me to, and it kills me, because it doesn't matter what he wants. He's a person who, like, gets dressed every other day. He eats *popcorn*, for Christ's sake. For dinner." She had her hands on her hips and she glared at the mower. "I don't even know how to turn this thing on."

I had seen her this way before. She possessed a special fury for machinery. When we were teenagers she stole her father's car, then left it at the gas station because she couldn't unscrew the gas cap. Back then, her indignation felt dangerous: she walked the sixteen blocks home, but it was like she had flown. She was frightening.

I was not sorry to see her shudder at the rust on her palms. Or clench her face and stamp at the ground. I wanted to be impressed by her, again.

But then she looked up, surprising me. Her eyes, impossibly, were red. "Amanda, can you help me with this?"

I was bewildered. "I'm in my socks."

"Gimme a break."

I moved off the stair. It was a hot day, and everything was wet—with the end of the morning's dew and the beginning of the humidity. I broke into a sweat, and Lora, I saw, had damp crescents at her armpits. We fiddled with gauges and unscrewed caps. Lora snapped impatient commands, and all the while I looked forward to the memory of this, the time when we would enjoy what we resented now.

"This is perfect," Lora snorted. "We are two perfectly useless people."

For a few seconds, she watched me tug at a strangled-looking pipe. Then she said, "Stop it, Amanda. I'm serious." She squinted her craggy face into the sun. "Just stop."

With most people in my life, I come to the end of myself pretty fast. I walk to my borders—where there's dinner on a dropleaf table, maybe small talk or sex—then wave politely and turn back. Lora made me sorry there wasn't anywhere better to go.

"We could hire someone to do the lawn." I knew I was trying too hard.

She threw up her hands at me, walked away. "Forget it. It doesn't matter. I'll tell him the lawn's mowed, and he'll have what he wants."

I did not sleep that night, not until almost morning. I lay unmoving on the couch for hours after Lora had gone to bed. With terrible slowness, the deep darkness in the room eventually began to change around me. At some indistinct point I noticed the grey-black shadows had taken on definite shapes and become furniture. Coat rack, exercise bike, coffee table. But where was the neighbor's barking dog? I wondered. The desolate predawn birds? It felt like paralysis, the way the night still went on and on, withholding details like birds and dogs till I wondered whether it could withhold me too. I slid one hand into my underpants. Leaned back. All anyone ever wants, I thought—feeling wretched and invisible at once—is someone to verify you're still here.

I woke the next morning with something in my mouth. I pulled a single dog hair from my tongue, shiny with spit, gray on one end and black on the other. I guessed it was midmorning at least. I lay and listened to the Sunday sounds, which made the house feel, suddenly, sad and dear: a talk show radio host in the kitchen, church bells down the street. Lora came in with a Styrofoam box, picking at last night's salad. "Morning." She waved a few glistening fingers.

I meant to leave by ten. I had packed my suitcase the night before and put it in the car, save my toiletries and a thank-you card. I believed in efficient departures.

Lora rubbed at her front tooth. "I should tell you, there's someone else here. Tom."

"Tom?" My mind went blank.

"Not *your* Tom, of course. A *guy* named Tom. He came over after you went to sleep. Tiptoed right past you."

Indignation caught in my throat. How could she invite a man over on my last night here?

"Don't look so scandalized!" Lora shook her head. I noticed she was wearing earrings, birds with turquoise eyes, and they lunged against her jaw. Her lips were a shade of purple she could not wear to Kohl's.

"Where is he now?" I looked into the kitchen and down the hall. I could not shake the feeling of conspiracy. They crowded illogically in my mind: some slack-eyed guy from a bar, Lora with her bruise-colored mouth, and poor old Tom, wasting away in the disease I'd wished upon him. I don't know which of them harassed me most.

"He's around. If you run into someone in the shower, that's probably him." Her smile was playful and mean, just short of confrontation.

I said, "Help me find my pants."

She said, narrowing her eyes, "You already *packed* them."

We didn't speak the rest of the morning. I padded in my cotton shorts down the driveway to the car, where I changed in the backseat with my packed bag—in case Lora's Tom came out from the bathroom or wherever he was—wiggling my thighs against the window crank and thrusting my hips to zip up the fly. Back inside, I slowed down when I passed Lora's room, listening. I knocked fearfully on the bathroom door. This man who was Tom could have any type of face. He could be any type of man, fretful and shy, a dumbass kid with nothing on his mind. I told myself this but I feared his gaze, as if he knew exactly how I'd promised and failed to love the other man with his name.

But there was no razor by the sink, no smeared steam on the mirrored walls. When the water was running, I thought I heard voices in the hall, but with the faucet off, there was nothing.

I sat down across from Lora at the kitchen table. She was painting her nails a Coke-can red, coating and blowing on them intermittently. With the cosmetics and jewelry, she looked young, haggard still, but working to impress someone.

"Is he here now?"

"Tom? He stepped out, I think."

"You *think*?"

"For coffee or something." She squinted hard at her work.

I also studied her hand: the bony knuckles, the fine network of wrinkles. It lay lightly on the table, waiting for someone to take it up.

"Will he come back?"

"Unless he gets run over by a truck."

I did not doubt his existence outright until later. I did not think she made him up until I was hundreds of miles down the road and the truth no longer seemed provable either way. For the moment, in the kitchen, I just watched Lora work, watched her dip the wet brush in the bottle and pluck it back out. She fretted over her nails with her usual carelessness, staining her cuticles and groaning at herself. She got three drips on the table. She coughed dramatically into the back of her hand, and a tiny red smear appeared on her face. Like a scar. Like a kiss.

When she caught my eye at last, I found my heart was pounding.

I pointed at the smudge on her face.

"What?" She looked almost shy. "What?"

The day Lora held me under water I'd been ignoring her. I'd been sitting on the dock, resentful of her ebullience in the water, self-conscious in my lumpy swimsuit. She'd been out swimming by herself all afternoon. Calling me from the ragged black center of the lake, diving under the dock from time to time, grabbing my ankles. When she unexpectedly tugged me down, a knife of water went up my nose. I remember seeing the flash of her white legs in the murk, a blaze of sun at the broken surface, and as she held me under, air bubbles moved over every surface of my skin. Swarming the backs of my arms, worming beneath my swimsuit and up my chest, fluttering in exquisite profusion up the length of my spine.

"What is it?" she asked now, again.

I took a breath, less sure.

Remembering the envelope in my hand, I leaned over and slid my prepared thank-you card across the tabletop.

Lora glanced down at it and up at me. Then, pivoting in her chair, she began drying her nails in the air. Bit by bit, as if her hands had gotten away from her, the gesture changed into a huge, sloppy, two-handed wave. She seemed to be laughing, hatefully, sorrowfully, her whole head tilting back on her neck. "Bye-bye! Bye-bye! Bye-bye!" she sang.

OLD HOUSE

The day I was sent home with pinkeye was the day my dad moved out. When I opened the back door, I saw him standing in the kitchen, all by himself, holding a leather suitcase with an X of frayed duct tape on one side like a mark for treasure. He was supposed to be at work. Eventually, he found something on the floor to hand me, my hockey stick probably, and said he was moving back to the "old house," a phrase I'd never heard him use before. He didn't ask about my bloodshot eye. I thought he must have meant the Old House in the swamp behind the school, the one with the boarded-up windows and collapsed porch. It was the only Old House that came to mind, and I was impressed and proud that my father was going there to live, envious even. I was eight, and I could not bring myself to reveal his location to anyone—even when my mom came home from work and begged me to tell her where he was. "He said something to you, Michael," she insisted. "I know he did!" I remember her face was blotchy and damp, and it made me think of something disturbing I shouldn't look at, like an old woman's saggy breast or a baby's full diaper. I hated the greasy lines on her forehead, the swollen stubble over her eyes.

"I can see by your expression that you're lying!" she accused me. "I've got pinkeye!" I yelled.

Later, when I was fourteen, I found out from my older sister that my father spent those two summer months he was away with his mistress at his parents' house in Wisconsin. In another conversation that same year, when I suggested the Old House as a good place to get drunk, a friend of a friend told me that the place in the swamp had burned down years ago, *back when we were six or seven*. So my Old House was gone long before my father's summer absence. These two facts came to me the way most of my adolescence did, as fundamentally unreal and insubstantial. I'd felt so close to my father those months he was gone, guilty and proud of myself for the secret I kept so well for him. Even after my sister's revelation, I half believed that the mistress story was just another part of my father's and my shared deception, a trick he'd played to keep his true location hidden. It felt like colluding with his lie when I said to my sister, "Really? He lived with Poppa and Grandma and his girlfriend? What a dick."

But in my heart, I admit, some part of me still believed that he spent that summer in the swamp, in the Old House behind the cottonwoods. He lived there with the high-stepping egrets and mucky sewer stench and molting brown cattails. He lived there, and all that summer I could have visited him on my bike, with a flashlight and a granola bar—but didn't, in case my mother followed me there and discovered him. I would not, would not betray him like that. I believed then, and still do I guess, that everything that came after in my adolescence, all those hours my father spent pulling me up from some lawn where I'd collapsed, all of that goddamned resigned patience he always had, he had because I had once kept his secret for him. It's funny how the mind works. I believed he thought he owed me something. I believed I must have earned his dogged, foolhardy trust.

*

I found myself thinking of the Old House again years later, long after I'd left home, in those intense, uncertain months when I was spending all my time with Liv. I met her my senior year in college, in the big Victorian boarding house where we both lived at the time. That house was battered and sloped—painted and painted over, like some hulking wooden boat. It had a sunk-ship look, wrecked against poplars. It was in a place that used to be suburbs but had become something else: part woods and overgrown lots, part boarded-up dry cleaners. The students who lived there were nontrads, transfers from community colleges, loners. We were either too poor or too scared to live alone, so five of us packed into the upper-story rooms and, I presume, masturbated as quietly as possible. We shared one bathroom, one finicky claw-foot bathtub, one cloudy mirror flecked with spit.

Our landlady was a white-haired old woman who kept albino rabbits in her backyard. Saturdays in the fall, Mrs. Crubin came knocking on our doors and recruited those of us who were available—usually it was just Liv and me, we were failed recluses for different reasons—to help clean out the hutches. I sprayed the wire mesh with thumbed hose water while Liv kept track of the rabbits on the lawn. She was thirty-six, gangly still, flat-chested as a runner. The rumor was that she had two children, girls, who'd gone to live with her mother when Liv returned to school after her divorce. As I lifted the dripping hutches to shake them out, I used to watch Liv watch me through the soapy wire mesh. Sometimes, she took a yellow-white rabbit in her arms and sang to it. I was twenty-three that fall, ready for anything, I thought. Liv sat cross-legged on the grass, toenails painted a chipped black, her face freckled, wrinkled around the eyes.

There were twelve rabbits altogether. *My apostles*, Mrs. Crubin called them. She had a cane of oiled rosewood, and once when we were standing in the yard she pulled the hooked end of that cane straight up, as if opening an umbrella. This revealed the bottom half of the cane as a rosewood sheath for a two-foot saber.

Mrs. Crubin had a passion for such secrets. Inside she showed us a beautiful faux Bible that was really a box for jewels. She opened a tarnished cake tin and showed us her Bible. As the sun sank behind the poplars, she led Liv and me into her dark back parlor, where she pulled little balled chains under Tiffany lamps. We were handed quivery orange mounds of cobbler. After pouring herbal tea, Mrs. Crubin showed us a peculiar lace doily that folded and buttoned and fashioned, finally, into a kind of glove. "Pretty?" she asked, putting it on. She was a New Christian, she explained, which, we were to understand, meant that she had an impregnable confidence in the deceptive nature of appearances. "The more one loves God, the nearer one draws to heaven."

I was a philosophy major, had encountered Swedenborg in lecture. "And the more you love yourself, the closer you get to hell?"

Mrs. Crubin was nod-nod-nodding. The thing that characterized those years, for me, was that I wanted an A from everybody, in all contexts.

Liv was a good student selectively. "Sounds like a rip-off of Buddhism to me."

Mrs. Crubin squinted over at her. "That's a pretty common misunderstanding." She seemed to pity Liv, and at the same time, want her confidence. Want mine. Her marbled blue eyes moved back and forth. "Did I tell you that I have been divorced, too? It wasn't a true spiritual marriage. My first husband qualified for the 1956 Olympics," she paused. "In *figure skating*."

A titter rose in my throat.

"Mmm?" Liv bit her lip, not quite sure if the joke was intentional.

But Mrs. Crubin, now, was laughing at her. "Ah. But my second husband and I will become one angel in heaven!"

"You will become—?" Liv started laughing just when Mrs. Crubin stopped.

"One angel in *heaven*, dear. He traded stocks before he passed. But he couldn't sleep unless I covered up his feet with a blanket.

He wouldn't do it for himself. I had to crawl down to the foot of the bed each night and do it for him, just so." Her eyes were shining. The little folds of skin on her throat trembled, like wet cloth. "My sweet, sweet man."

Mrs. Crubin was barely out of the room with our plates before Liv had opened the faux Bible back up and started pawing through the tangled beaded necklaces. "She seems to love herself just fine," Liv whispered. "Look at this all shit she has."

I tsked. "So far away from heaven, right?"

Liv grinned. "Hell. We're in hell, basically."

*

For a long time, Mrs. Crubin was our private game. I think we both looked forward to Saturday nights, so Liv could egg Mrs. Crubin on and get her to tell us about her figure skater and her economist, her beau and her bull, she called them, both of whom were still very vivid to her—even though, Mrs. Crubin said, her second husband had been taken to a nursing home by his children years before he finally passed. "How did he die?" Liv would sometimes ask, to provoke her. He *hadn't* died, Mrs. Crubin reminded her. The essential person, she said, is actually still alive. "Like in heaven," Liv pressed. Mrs. Crubin smiled patiently. Yes, she said, but it's important to remember that both heaven and hell are relative states of proximity to Love.

Sometimes Mrs. Crubin read us passages from Swedenborg's writings to clarify the points she was making, rickety lines of prose written more than two hundred years ago in Latin. When she did this, I'd often lose the thread of the conversation, but Liv—who had a better memory, who was better than me at most things—would ask specific, discriminating, elaborate questions. Later when she saw me in the hallway, she'd quote from these passages as if they were lines from her favorite movies. Or as if they were a private language she'd mastered, along with Hindi, her major, for our mutual delectation. I tried to make her effort seem worth it.

Once outside the bathroom, for instance, she reached out her hand and stroked my newly shaved chin. Suggestively, mischievously. "Everything that is perceived and felt in the body finds its or-i-gin in its spiritual counterpart because it comes from our, um, intellect and volition."

I paused, damp towel around my hips. Dripping on the floorboards. "*Intellect and Volition*, the lost, last novel of Jane Austen."

"Ha," she said, closing the bathroom door.

I admit I felt lucky to have Mrs. Crubin at first, to have such a convenient way to bridge awkward moments like this with Liv, who could be intimidating. We thought of Mrs. Crubin as essentially harmless, decorous to the point of absurdity. She was impressive in her ability to transport another century into the house, to treat the guy who mowed her lawn and the woman who brought her meals like live-in servants. So when was it that I started to feel differently? Probably it wasn't until after Mrs. Crubin's second or third stroke, because the effects of the first ones in October and November were hardly noticeable. She was a little slower in her speech, a little more slumped when she sat in her scrolled armchair in the parlor, as if her organs had slid to one side of her body. I started noticing a uriney stench when I got too close, and sometimes her mouth would go slack as a mask and leak lines of white drool. But that was later on. In the beginning, she was our toy.

*

After Mrs. Crubin fed us cobbler those early September nights, after she showed us her faux Bible and went to bed, we had the house to ourselves. The other students in the house all had weekend jobs or dates or drunk parties at the lake where the fraternities owned boathouses. I remember sitting with Liv among those horned antiques in Mrs. Crubin's parlor, lingering over the last gelatinous, sweet bites of cobbler. The setting was ridiculous, like something out of Oscar Wilde, but on the third or fourth Saturday, Liv just stepped over the mahogany coffee table and plopped down next to me on the loveseat.

There was never any fuss about her. "You're staring at me," she said.

I suppose I must have seemed very young to her then, but I'd felt older than everyone else my age for so long that I believed we had something in common. That night Liv told me stories about India, where she wanted to live, and anecdotes about the little Iron Range town, Eveleth, where she grew up. "They called it the Taconite Capital of the World," she told me. "What, Mumbai?" I said. She flicked my arm with a finger. She leaned in and kissed my mouth. She was sticky with cobbler, both her lips and her fingers, and she held her long staticky hair away from our faces with one hand.

"Hold this a sec," she said—meaning her hair—so I did, while she dug in her pocket for an elastic. She retrieved her hair from me, ponytailed it back. Then she unbuckled my pants and we clumsily fucked. Silk sofa pillows slid one by one to the floor. Liv's hands clamped my T-shirted chest.

"You okay?" she asked when we were done. Ponytail swinging.

I remember trying to keep Mrs. Crubin's loveseat as clean as possible, standing up in an awkward, armless way that required me to arch my back while clutching my pants.

"Yup," I assured her. Then, and every time after that, she'd have a grin ready for me, one I believed, incorrectly perhaps, I'd earned by being tractable, nonchalant, and grateful.

*

Surely there were nights that fall when I lay alone on my mattress in the dark, feeling sorry for myself and impatient with Liv for being gone so much, for spending so many late nights in the library. And surely there were other students in Mrs. Crubin's house who had faces, names, and complications themselves. When I ran into them, no doubt, I resented them their radio alarms, their stubbed-out cigarettes in the bathroom sink. I'm sure I resented their presence in that house that, increasingly, started to seem like Liv's and mine alone. We were inhabitants, protagonists. They were intruders.

But most of those details are gone to me now. What I remember clearly is that by the end of fall semester I'd abandoned my second-floor room and shoved my mattress up the stairs to Liv's third-floor turret. I lined up my single mattress next to hers and covered the whole thing with a wool blanket. My desk fit perfectly in the octagonal corner, and that's where I sat in the short winter afternoons watching the backyard trees drop clumps of snow into the drifts below. A volunteer from the Humane Society came by on a blustery afternoon before Christmas and collected all twelve apostles from the backyard, shoving them one by one into cardboard boxes. I watched anxiously through the leaded glass window. I was surprised at how roughly that woman in her long puffy coat handled them, as if she were packing up laundry or something—as if gentleness with animals didn't count unless someone else was watching. I had the impulse to climb down the stairs, let her know she'd been seen. Then she drove off in a cloud of exhaust and I was relieved. Though I had gotten part-time work at a pizzeria over break, it was a job that required almost nothing from me—and I remember feeling pleasantly adrift in those early winter weeks, increasingly unnecessary to anyone but Liv, who called me her Victim.

"Victim," she'd say, nudging me awake when she got home late from the library. "Come here."

I got up and followed her. Sometimes she wanted to shove open the leaded glass window and let a little stinging snow blow in. She wanted to be shivering, goose-pimpled. She wanted to warm my shriveled cock with her mouth. "I like the word 'screw,'" she'd whisper in the awful cold. "I like the word 'fuck,' but every other word for sex is a joke, isn't it?" I never spoke at times like this out of fear of using one of the many words that turned her off, by accident. "'*Do* it,'" she mocked, "'*sleep* with,' 'make *love*'?" If it was late enough that it was morning, she sometimes led me in my groggy state to the shared bathroom down the hall, or to the hallway, or to the stairwell. She liked semipublic places. She liked almost getting caught, playing with me in doorways. Once I leaned back against the huge, curved banister in the hallway while she sucked me off, another of the tenants blow-drying her hair in the bathroom five feet away. "'Intercourse,'" Liv lifted her head to say—just when the whir of the dryer cut off. "From the Old French, meaning 'commerce.'"

The bathroom door opened. We scurried up the stairs.

Before long the icicles outside all the windows were as fat as human thighs. Winter deepened. The radiators were scorching to the skin if you touched them. The stairwell left splinters if you weren't careful, and the kitchen linoleum was gummy against our backs from years of unwashed grime. When I helped her up at the end that time, the bare skin on her back made a kissing sound that made my own skin crawl. "That was hot," I said, trying to sound satisfied, enthusiastic. What I didn't, or couldn't, admit to her was that I liked our cozy turret best. I liked our two mattresses that took up most of the room and the big wool blanket over both of us. I liked those rare weekend mornings when we stayed in bed, when we lay naked together and watched the weak winter sun shovel squares of light across the stucco wall. On those mornings I could hear the whole house shifting beneath us, pipes popping, people coming and going, water running, and it was so exquisite to fuck leisurely like that, to screw in private slow motion, perched atop it all.

*

"What do you think Mrs. Crubin would say," Liv asked me once, "if she knew?" I shrugged. The truth was by then, by winter, we didn't have to deal with Mrs. Crubin very much anymore because of her deteriorating health. But we did occasionally. On New Year's Eve we forced ourselves. We made a pot of oily chili on our hotplate upstairs and carried the leftovers with our rent checks down to Mrs. Crubin, who could no longer walk—even with her cane—who was now looked over by paid caretakers in shifts. For the caretakers' convenience, I guess, a hospital bed had been set up in the parlor among her whorled cabinets and side tables. We followed one of these caretakers in with New Year's napkins, Tabasco sauce. Half sitting up in bed, Mrs. Crubin wore a long-sleeved sweater dress in pilled coral.

"Happy New Year!" Liv said.

Mrs. Crubin said, "Nrrrrrminnihhppaa."

The blue-haired nurse at her bedside bustled about, unconcerned. She tucked a New Year's napkin under Mrs. Crubin's chin, plunked a plastic spoon in Liv's opened Tupperware of chili. "Do you want to feed her tonight? She'd like that, I bet. What a nice idea. Yum, yum, yum."

The nurse patted Mrs. Crubin's belly, and Mrs. Crubin's eyes went wide.

"Umm," I said, backing up.

Liv didn't balk. "Maybe in a little bit. Let's give it a minute." At the side table, she pushed aside some animal figurines and candlesticks to make room for the sweating Tupperware in her hands. "I know, I know, I know. Let's watch the ball drop." She gestured for me to turn on the black-and-white television in the corner. "Let's watch that party they do at Times Square. Mrs. Crubin, you'd like to see that, wouldn't you?" Liv's voice had taken on a formal quality I'd never heard her use before, a glittery, almost girlish lilt. It surprised me how much I appreciated the effort she made, the performance of sincerity for Mrs. Crubin's sake.

So for a couple of hours, maybe more, we sat together in the dim parlor—Nurse, Liv, Mrs. Crubin, and I—and listened to dogs bark outside, and watched the crowds heave in Times Square, and eventually heard the roar across the country. "Five, four, three, two," Liv said, taking my hand. She and I were sitting on the tiniest of Mrs. Crubin's loveseats, the one with armrests carved to look like braided ropes. Mrs. Crubin and the caretaker were either absorbed in the festivities on TV or fast asleep. They were silent in the furnitured dark behind us. I remember feeling a dense ache of ownership as that ball descended, a strange proprietary joy at seeing Liv's unexpected kindness to Mrs. Crubin that night, her intuitive sense of the old lady's—what? Dignity. She's truly a good person, I thought. And though I hadn't had any particular reason to think this before, I felt I must have sensed it anyhow, that this reflected well on me, too.

*

A little while later, upstairs in our turret, something small and hard tumbled to the mattress when I pulled off Liv's sweatshirt. She was wet-lipped, panting. The object looked like a rooster. It had iridescent purple plumage in a fan around its ceramic neck, and it lay on its side in the sheets as we looked down at it. Red claw facing us. "Oh, yeah!" Liv laughed. "Hey, look—"

She found a switch behind its plumage and swung open its head. Inside its hollow ceramic body were a bunch of old yellowed toothpicks. "Isn't this awful?" she asked, pinching up a pick. "I know. I should feel bad about taking it."

"You should," I said, uneasily. I recognized it as one of Mrs. Crubin's majolica figurines from the parlor, one from the collection of trinkets she'd shown us with such ceremony in the fall when we'd talked about the afterlife and eaten cobbler together.

Liv grinned. "You feel bad *for* me, how about that?" She planted a kiss on the tip of my nose like a princess doing, or undoing, a spell. "There! You be Guilt. I'll be Bad Behavior. We'll be a division of labor."

"Liv—"

"Come *on*, Michael, what use is it to her anymore? She doesn't have any family, clearly. All that crap of hers will just end up getting hauled off, like the rabbits were. It'll all end up at Goodwill." She opened and closed the rooster head like a mouth. "Isn't this just hideous? Wouldn't my girls get a kick out of it?"

I felt an unexpected clutch of love for her then. "Let me meet your kids."

"The girls?" She worked the toothpick back into its little bundle. She closed the rooster head. Opened it again. "They're little witches, they're in a stage." She seemed pleased by this answer. "They hate all men-shaped people."

"I'm serious."

"You know a lot about kids, Michael?"

"My sister has a five-year-old—"

She leaned over me to set the majolica rooster on the concrete-block shelf beside her books. Pursed her lips at me, ruffled my hair. "Oh, Michael, you were a big babysitter, probably, when you were a teenager. When you were drunk every night and your daddy wiped the sick off you—"

I stiffened under the lightness of her hand. "That's not what I said—"

"—or when you spent all those months in rehab? And dropped out of school? I'm sure you know everything there is to know about being a good parent? I mean, I'm sure it all comes naturally to you."

"That's not fair."

*

But it was. I had told her all that shit because I thought if I did she might start to see me as more than just a nerdy kid with a thing for older women. I'd felt protective, almost proud, of the story of driving the car into the pond or of the time my dad found me collapsed behind the shed one particularly bad night. I'd explained to Liv how my dad had rolled me carefully onto his overcoat and dragged me up the hill to the house. I couldn't remember much from that episode, of course, but I did remember how soft his face looked as he struggled with my weight, as if there weren't any bones left beneath the skin. Freed in this way, his face had moved through a thousand instantaneous, unfamiliar expressions. Revulsion, pity, love. I told Liv this. I explained how marvelous it had been to see him that way—my dad, who was usually so cool and removed.

I told Liv these stories, and others, because I believed we had something in common, a past, which made us both a little remote in the lives we'd chosen. We both had done well in school—were our professors' favorite students—because we tried too hard to prove we belonged. This is how I understood her at first. She'd done Hindi and I chose philosophy, both uselessly complex, like those inflated, perverse muscles body builders cultivate in their wrists and necks and pectorals. I wanted her to see that I could understand how much a burden that intelligence was, how it wasn't intelligence at all, not really, but an acute sensitivity to the expectations of others.

*

But Liv wasn't as relieved about the prospect of finishing college as I was. As the spring semester wore on, she finagled a second translating job from another of her professors. My interest in philosophy had fallen off that spring, and I turned everything in unedited and early. But Liv stayed up translating at her desk long after I went to bed, hunched in a little ring of light under her desk lamp in the corner. She planned to graduate with honors. When the yellow tassels arrived in a hive-like coil in the mail, I was surprised to see her unwind them right away and drape them unironically over her shoulders. In May, she won a grant to work on archival documents in Delhi the next fall.

"It's a free ride!" she exclaimed the warm spring night she told me about it.

We were eating dinner at Liv's desk, perched uneasily on plastic folding chairs. I'd wedged open the leaded glass window with a book, and I remember hearing one of the caretakers taking out the trash down below—dragging a metal can across the driveway—in the long silence that opened up between us.

"But you're not really thinking of going?"

I assumed Liv would stay around for her children, at least, whom she visited one weekend each month. I pointed that out. I said I expected that a year away from one's children—"one's children," I really said that—would be unthinkable in her position.

"What position is that?" She stood up. Because she was sweating and the folding chair was light, it stuck for a moment to her thighs before thudding to the floor. "Do you mean I should not do this thing, take advantage of this opportunity, because I have kids? Because—" She shook her head in disbelief. "I slept with a guy when I was eighteen, and that guy didn't like the feel of condoms? I think *that's* the unthinkable thing, if you want to know the truth. That's the thing I can never, ever get my mind around. *This* is pretty thinkable, actually."

"I get it. Okay, okay," I said, trying to calm her back down. I'd made two chicken potpies in Mrs. Crubin's oven that night. I'd snuck down the stairs and past the parlor door in my socks, avoided one of the caretakers who was heading out by hovering in a shadowy spot near the basement stairs. I'd wanted us to have a real dinner together for once. It was nearly summer! I'd lit a candle.

So I changed the subject. I poked holes in the crust of my potpie, warned Liv to do the same. "They're hot!" I told her, tenderly waving away her steam.

She sat down again. Then pried the whole crust back at once, like a lid. Steam poured over her plate. "I've eaten chicken pot pies before, Michael. I *grew up* on frozen pot pies, remember?"

*

How could I remember that? When she talked like that I believed that she was really talking to someone else—her husband, the ex—who must have known a great deal about her pot-pie childhood. All I knew was that one Friday a month she took an overnight bus to Eveleth. That's where Liv's teenage daughters lived with her mother in a house on Elbow Creek. She came home Sunday nights with crumb cake wrapped in foil and a mildewy smell—the smell of moldy carpets and sweating walls, of basements—and for the first day or two she was back, she skirted over me, over everything. She was studiously serene, distracted. She did laundry, wrote out bills. She bent her thumbnail back as if it were on a hinge, exposing and covering again the spongy white cuticle.

Sometimes, I admit, I took her thumb into my mouth and did the bad deed for her, bit the nail off. I pretended, with obscure moaning, that it was something sexual I liked, some weird oral fetish. Liv believed that men did things for all kinds of implausible erotic reasons. But really I just wanted her to be done worrying. And also, maybe, I wanted to hurt her.

*

"Marry me," I blurted one night, pulling her across the mattresses and into my arms.

The words surprised us both, I think. We fishtailed for a moment between solemnity and joke. She squirmed in my arms.

"Yeah, right!" Liv laughed, then was silent for a long time. I could feel her heart beating, through her back and in my ribcage, before I realized it was mine. Finally: "Actually, that's not nice, Michael."

"What?" I spoke into her hair. "Asking you to be my wife, my betrothed, my life partner?" I was half playing, half hurt. "It seems pretty nice to me. I'm a pretty nice guy, if you haven't noticed."

She wiggled out of my grasp. "If by 'nice' you mean a little judgmental—yes, I have in fact noticed that. You're always acting like you're this amazingly decent person, like you're just sort of tolerating everybody else, somehow. Me."

"I'm trying to make you feel better! I'm trying to make you feel good!"

She curled up against the wall. "You're trying to make *yourself* feel better."

*

But by then I believed she needed me and just couldn't bear to acknowledge it. I'd come by degrees to know things about Liv's body and predilections, though she always acted like she was introducing me to everything for the first time, to all her elaborate, idiosyncratic preferences. I knew, for instance, that she liked to have her right leg bent up when we fucked, the bright red knob of her knee tucked near her ear. And I knew to keep my eyes open. I knew how and when to help her pull her hair away from her face so she could focus on what she was doing. She couldn't stand hair in her face, would lose all interest if she had to scrape a single strand from her mouth with a finger. "That's enough," she'd say. "That's over." Within a few months, I'd learned how to hold her hair in a ponytail, wind it into a bun, mash it between my teeth when I came in her from behind.

Or, when she crawled around on her knees and blew on my erection like a candle, I knew to let her. She kissed the head and nuzzled it with her chin, and that was fine by me. I let her rub her nose against it. I let her say: "I'm going to huff and puff and blow your house in!" Did she laugh then? I decided it was alright if she did. Once she made me put on her panties afterward, snapping the tight elastic across my pubic hair, and it was—all of it—worth trying, I felt. I was receptive, game, compliant, calm. Indulgent. By late May, it occurred to me that we just needed to find some new way or place, some fresh position or approach, that would inevitably catapult us from this stage to the next. It felt like a project to be working on it like this together, interesting and absorbing work, almost wholesome.

*

Often in those early summer nights, we'd hear a burbling, singing sound coming up the stairway. Rising through the dark, silent house.

Mrs. Crubin, of course.

"*Hmmploooha,*" Liv mimicked, nailing the aspirated "p," the secondary stress, the rising intonation. We were under a sheet, naked, and Liv's ribs in my arms heaved in silent laughter. "*Bhhlmmpahak!*" Her pronunciation was eerily perfect. She had a good ear.

Then, whispering: "What's the 'spiritual counterpart' for drooling, do you think?" Her voice was warm against my neck, a tight, frenzied whirlpool of heat. "What is your relative proximity to Love when you can't control your bladder?"

"Ha," I said, bending away from her breath. Feeling the warm stucco wall rise up beside me, the rough, rounded edge of the mattress.

Other than Mrs. Crubin and the occasionally murmuring nurses, the house was perfectly quiet. By then Liv and I were the only tenants left. The others vacated in April and May when classes let out, breaking their leases, taking menial cashiering jobs in the little Midwest towns where they were born.

*

One humid evening around this time, I crept downstairs at dusk. Liv was gone—at another departmental function, another school thing—and I'd been halfheartedly filling out applications for summer jobs at camps and libraries. Queasy with the heat of the house, I planned to filch a few cubes of ice from the freezer for my mug of Coke. I could hear a voice murmuring in the parlor as I passed, someone going: "First one arm, then the other." In the kitchen, the ice cubes grew slick in my hands as I gently lowered them to my mug. I was very quiet as I closed the freezer door, and even so, I heard shoes unsticking from the linoleum behind me. I turned.

"Excuse me?" This caretaker was unfamiliar to me, young. "Could you lend a hand?"

She must have mistaken me for family, because she started explaining that the next caretaker would be here in an hour. "Would you mind making sure she's comfortable? Just till Tanya arrives?"

Did I look nervous to her?

"She's sleeping now," the young nurse soothed. She was maybe pretty, and she appeared practiced at using this possibility to her advantage. A tuft of strawberry blonde hair fell in front of her blinking green eyes. "Come on in. I'll just show you what to do real quick if she needs something."

The black-and-white TV in the corner was on. The shades were closed. I realized then that I hadn't been in the parlor since winter, since New Year's. The furniture in the room had settled more completely into its rummage-sale look, everything shoved together at awkward, acute angles. The small majolica figurines on the tables were knotted in indecipherable shadows.

I carefully avoided looking at Mrs. Crubin in her bed. The nurse whispered me through adjusting her pillow and refilling her water cup with its crooked straw, and all the while I stayed at the far side of the room near the door. "Otherwise, you just make yourself comfortable," the nurse said. "Okay?"

"Okay." I made a point of blandly reassuring her. I assumed I would bail the moment the caretaker left, but I didn't. I was still the guy who wanted, in some aching, irrational way, an A in everything anyone asked of me.

So I sat down on the loveseat farthest from the hospital bed. To my confusion and delight, the winter Olympics were on TV. What channel was this? I wondered vaguely. I'd read about the results in the paper months ago, but here they were replaying the winter Olympics in June. I sank into the cool silk of the claw-foot loveseat to watch them, the ski-jumping men floating ominously as raptors, strumming the air with one hand. I watched overturned bobsleds grind men's heads as they plummeted down the track. I watched Apolo Ohno take the ice.

"He wins." Someone touched my shoulder from behind, so I started. Liv's fingers on my neck were cold, though the room was stuffy and warm, airless. She slunk around the little couch, shrugged out of her backpack.

"Apolo Ohno? What are you—"

Just as I was about to ask Liv what she was doing here, how she knew where I'd be, Mrs. Crubin began calling out to us.

"Goomlhaa! Hmmoolpaa!"

Curling up beside me on the silk, Liv kissed my neck.

"We should go see what she needs," I said. "I was told—"

"*Hmmoolpaa*," she murmured. "Which means, in New Christian, she wants us to stay right here and make out. I've been brushing up on my vocabulary and pronunciation. That's what she's trying to say."

I stood up. "No, really. I'm supposed to see—"

Liv frowned, then smiled. "Yes, let's."

She took my hand and led me in a winding path through the jumble of furniture across the shadowy room to where a red rose nightlight glowed from the wall. The old lady was tucked under white sheets, and her neck lifted up her head when we drew closer. I saw the drapery of her braid of hair unraveling down her night-gowned arm. I saw the flash of her gray tongue, the whites of her eyes.

"Mrs. Crubin?" I said.

When I looked for Liv, I saw she was on her knees in front of me.

"No."

"What, Michael?" She was unzipping my pants. She was whispering: "What can she do? What can she say? Anyways, none of this is real to her, remember—"

I started to push her away.

"We're just—appearances of Love, right? We'll make one angel for her."

Her voice was excited, husky with malice. Then she had my cock in her mouth. I shoved her back, fumbling with the zipper on my pants, but—how can this be explained?—even as I did, I felt the thrill of unexplored possibility. It occurred to me that this might be what we'd been working toward all these months, the experience that would finally bind us together.

"Come on," Liv said. "You be Bad Behavior."

"No."

"I'll be Guilt." She twisted around and shot a glance at Mrs. Crubin over her shoulder, and it was such a wretched look, filled with such unguarded misery, that something unlatched in my body and a familiar feeling flooded through me. It was the feeling that used to come over me only when I was high or really drunk—not that nothing mattered, but that everything did the exact same amount. Not just me spinning Liv against the wall and hiking up her skirt, but also the way her wrist bone pressed against my forehead and the way her eyelid twitched and the sound of our skin sticking and pulling apart. There was no differentiating one thing from another, no distinguishing the frost-like pattern of the wallpaper from the moaning of the old lady beside us from my dad's face as he dragged me over the lawn, from his love and his disgust, from the big pulsing vein now visible in Liv's forehead. It was all the same thing.

Afterward, Liv pulled down her skirt and plucked out the rose nightlight from the socket with a little crack.

In the dark, we started giggling. Then stopped. Mrs. Crubin was quiet, there was no sound, and I thought—with a sudden chill, like being splashed—maybe she died. Maybe she's dead. But then she was gurgling again, so we closed the heavy parlor doors behind us and crept up the stairs.

*

I make that seem like the big event. I make it seem like something was settled between us after that, that when we went to barbeques or the store or whatever, we introduced ourselves as a couple. That it had worked. And we did go on for several more months. And the same things we did before—study, cook, take the bus—did feel different, strange, like when you travel somewhere new and come back and home feels provisional for a while, imperceptibly charged with the overwhelming knowledge of the unfamiliar place you've just been. There seemed to arise between Liv and me an awareness that hadn't been there before, an electric, ineffable understanding. Without discussing it, I came to recognize that I would follow her to India if she accepted the grant. It seemed almost beyond talking about, a decision that was long since settled between us. I looked into getting a visa, went to the library and found a book on conversational Hindi, told my dad when he asked what I was doing after graduation that I probably was going abroad. I got the vaccinations. I looked into plane tickets.

But when she announced in September that she was going to go up to Eveleth to say "'bye to the girls" before her flight to Mumbai, there was a blank between us, a pause, and I didn't say I would go with her. I drove her to the bus station and bought her lunch, a burrito. I lifted her bags into the compartment under the bus, and when she waved down from her tinted window I felt an unclenching in my chest as if I were really sad to see her go. I waved until the bus had disappeared in the surge of traffic, and it was only when I was driving down the shaded streets by myself that I found I could hardly stand to think of her. And it was only weeks later, when my dad asked me about my upcoming trip abroad, that I felt such a stunning repugnance at the thought that my skin seemed to slide against my bones when I moved the phone from one hand to the other. "I don't know what you're talking about," I said. "I've got a new apartment, a part-time job at the library."

And Mrs. Crubin? To my knowledge, she may still be alive.

LEARNING TO WORK WITH YOUR HANDS

I never knew him well and never will: old spitting man, man in suspenders. Anyhow, everyone's grandfather is like this. He has purple lips and yellow teeth. He wears ball caps from extinct teams, one ear tucked in and one folded out at a perfect right angle. When I turned fourteen, he gave me a model of the Liberty Bell, mistaking my curiosity about him, my questions about his soldier days, for patriotism. He admired citizens, not granddaughters. The bell had a tiny brass clapper that rattled in the dome like a mint in a candy tin. I attached it to the dog's collar and let her be the patriot between us, the one who stayed with my grandfather in the long afternoons and licked his knuckles.

The day they lifted him up and carried him from our house to the stretcher on the porch, I put my arms around the dog to keep her out of the way. She smelled of kitty litter. She reared her head, so I grabbed her ears and pulled hard, watching the skin on the top of her skull slide back like a hood. A red ambulance light swept through the room. My parents exchanged irritable commands, saying, "Get his arms up! Take off his hat!" My grandfather held on to the front door molding and had to be pried away by a male EMT. The EMT smoothed Grandpa's forehead, murmuring, "There you are, there you are," like a mother after a bad dream. "Moron," Grandpa said, but they were already out on the driveway, and someone was yelling something about retrieving his kicked-off shoe.

That's when our house was still painted a funny yellow color, like the feathers of a bird at a pet store. Before Grandpa left, my mother was like a visitor here. She slid between politeness for my grandfather's sake and the sort of despair where you start a hobby. She collected miniatures, but not dollhouses. She had oriental carpets the size of postcards and a claw-foot bathtub where we put our soap. After Grandpa left, she packed up room after tiny room in a red tackle box. I watched her fit porcelain cakes under minuscule lounge cushions, wrap lamps in the cloth napkins she used for guests. She put on mascara and squinted at herself in the mirror the way the girls at school did, as if the image made her heartsick. She didn't have a car, so Dad and I drove her to her Pilates instructor's house where there was a hot tub and a futon for her in the converted garage she'd rented. I thought she would cry. I wanted her to cry, so we could all feel her long inertia was worth something. Instead she went right over to the hot tub and stuck her finger in, rolling her eyes to the ceiling and clicking her tongue. She took my hand and dunked it in the water, saying, *Feel this*.

Before Grandpa left, our street was called Fifth Avenue South, but after he was gone it changed to Green Mountain Road. They put in a golf course in the field next door, with putting greens like round carpets and a sprinkler system that watered our garage. Within a few months, all our neighbors sold their houses to real estate brokers from the Cities. Kitty Roster, who'd been my friend since we were babies together, called the brokers the Hippie Hitlers because they had moustaches and sandaled feet. The Rosters sold their stucco house and bought a mobile home on the lake, with a dock on floaters and a pontoon boat. A sign in the shape of a mountain appeared where their house used to be.

The last time I talked to Kitty was Memorial Day. The Rosters invited me for a ride in their new boat. They were sorry for me because my father was too proud to sell our house, even for twice the money Grandpa paid for it. When I got to the lake, the Rosters filled a cooler with Diet Cokes and we sputtered to a place in the water where the lily pads thinned. Kitty's mother rubbed oil on our backs. Kitty's brother and father squinted silently at fishing lures. Kitty and I dangled our legs in the lake, watching skiers hunch over their handles and sprawl into nests of foam. After a while, I touched Kitty's greasy leg. "I'm hungry," I whispered to her. She spread herself out flat on the green felt floor: "Then eat."

"What?" I asked. "Your dad's crawdads?"

She looked at me like she'd raised me from a child, and only now did it occur to her we weren't related.

On Green Mountain Road, my father still dragged out screens in the spring to replace the winter storm windows. When the golfers came after lost balls, my father shook out the screens in the sun and waved a single hand at them. They prodded our tomato seedlings with clubs. My father looked at them like he was sorry they were alive. He climbed up a ladder and pulled out the storm windows one by one, opening up the house as if it were a tent he could dismantle if he chose to. He had me stand beneath the ladder and take the panes of glass: heavy, smudged by the dog's nose, cold against my face. My arms were barely long enough to span the width of them.

I was fifteen years old and ninety-six pounds. I had a long, long neck covered in a fine white down and big red hands like a middle-aged man. That summer my father put me to work dragging the lawnmower over the dandelions and painting the house white. I liked the bright chemical scent of the paint, the way the brush made a kissing sound on certain surfaces. Up and down the block, construction crews were driving bulldozers into our neighbors' houses. Like the golfers, these men wore sunglasses and gloves. It embarrassed them to see a teenage girl with a paintbrush and a sunburn. They said to me, "Where's your daddy?" and "Shouldn't you be at camp or something?" And once, "We should get one like that for ourselves. Do you think the boss'd go for it? A little girl?"

That summer, I let my father buy me a used bike, and crouched with him while he unstrung the chain and ran his finger along its greasy knobs. I didn't tell him the girls from school had begun sneering at bikes, talking about the cars they would drive when they got their permits. I let my father take me to his barber, where a parrot with blue claws perched on the mirror and said, *Up, up and away.* The barber did my father while the barber's son did me. He seemed sorry about what he would do. He said, *You'll be alright,* putting one finger on the very top of my head as if determining my axis. I liked how his breath smelled, and later when I saw my reflection in the car window, I decided it was fine. I looked like one of those angels you see on Christmas cards: serene, boyish, alien.

In early June, my father took me for coffee. We sat at the counter in a room called Gary's that was a café in the morning and a bar at night. After coffee, my father wanted eggs and Cokes, and then we left and crossed the river bridge so he could show me the place on the courthouse steps where an Indian cut off both his hands. To keep from being shackled, my father said.

"Problem was, after he got one hand off, what's he to do with the other? Think about it. Same hand's got to chop and be chopped."

I knew I needed to be brutal and clever all at once. My father fought in Vietnam and understood the intricacies of mutilation. "He threw the hatchet up in the air and let it fall on his wrist."

He shook his head. "Cassie. This isn't a movie I'm talking about."

He turned and walked up the stairs.

"Okay, then." I caught up with my father. "Mr. Indian, he's fingering his hatchet and thinking, 'How do I kill these two birds at once?' Wait. Who let him keep a weapon, anyway?" The marble was so white with sun, I stumbled and missed a step.

"Let's go," my father said.

"I'm going," I said back.

It wasn't that he was scornful. He was just busy unwrapping a gray stick of gum. I think a teenage daughter must be like one of those lawn ornaments everybody has, one of those grotesque little gnomes that are so useless and absurd you don't even need to look at them.

"How about this. He propped the hatchet up and fell on it."

"Cassie," he sighed. "You're not thinking of it right."

That was the summer one of the junior girls slit her wrists in a porta-potty by the river. Nona Allen was one of those skulky, quiet kids so tall she'd made the male teachers nervous. They'd talked to her impatiently, as if she had been insubordinate by growing so large. After Nona's death they felt bad about this, saying, *She had such a marvelous mind.* They remembered how she'd been good at math, how she'd taken the city bus to the technical college after homeroom. "We shall never know what she was capable of," the principal declared at her memorial service. He paused to adjust the microphone on his collar, making the room ring. I sat next to my father, who was opening and closing a Bible on his knee.

My mother was there, too. She remembered Nona fondly from when she used to come over, years ago, and entertain me and Kitty Roster while my mother took baths or shopped. Mom met us outside the funeral parlor after the service, dressed for a summer outing in a blue skirt and high heels. Beneath her eyes, she had two skin-colored tapes that didn't match her face, which was splotchy-red and tight—from all those hours in the hot tub, I guess.

"A shame," she said, touching the bridge of her nose.

My father kissed her red cheek and walked to the car.

The next girl people talked about was a senior, and she just disappeared for a while, so there was speculation about pregnancy, anorexia. Then I spotted her again in the middle of July, wrapped in a beach towel outside the new pool. Julie had been ferocious and unpopular in school, winning track races and scholarships for college. But when I saw her that summer—outside the pool, nibbling bagels in the coffee shop—she looked fragile and spent. All her parts were so delicately fastened, her wispy hair, her new wasted limbs.

Pneumonia, people said. *She coughed up blood for weeks.* The senior girls decided to dedicate the first summer pool party to her.

One of these seniors, a girl I used to play softball with, stopped me at Eller's Market in mid-June. Annie was working the checkout line, and I didn't recognize her until she set a cabbage on her palm and made a wind-up gesture. I lifted up my hands. She grinned and put the cabbage on the scale, nicking a few buttons with her fingertips.

"So, Cassandra." Her eyes slid up from the register. She looked tired, her curled bangs catching on her eyebrows. I couldn't remember what color her hair used to be, but now it was maroon as a plum. "What's up?"

"Nothing much."

"You're starting high school, right?"

"Yep." I paid and looped plastic bags around my wrist.

I started to turn away, but Annie was smiling in such an expectant way that I thought she needed something else from me. She said, "So. See you?"

When I didn't answer, she wrapped her hands up in her apron like a muff. A line was growing at the register.

She shifted tactics. "*Seriously*, Cassandra. We should, like, hang out or something." She waited for me to agree, and when I didn't, she went on, almost irritably. "There's this pool party for Julie— you know Julie?—tomorrow. Everyone will be there."

She raised her eyebrows. I couldn't understand why she was smiling so hard. I stared at her for a second, and it was then that I understood we were playing a game: the one where girls defeat and own each other through public acts of kindness.

I gripped my bags. "I've got work."

"Come after!" she persisted.

I stood my ground, shrugged.

She was offended. "You should see Julie!" she accused. "She's so sick she can barely lift her head!"

By midsummer, the neighborhood was quiet and dense with new houses: ranches with three-car garages, Greek columns on the front stoops. The contractors packed up their bulldozers and trailers and got out of town. Realtors in tight skirts wedged FOR SALE signs in the mud. They parked their tiny, foreign cars on the street, snapping pictures with digital cameras. From the roof of my father's house, I could see them cleaning their heels on the black-tar driveways. They never looked up at me. I crouched by the chimney with a crowbar, red scabs on my knees. I plucked out flat nails one by one, then shoved the crowbar deep into the tarry skin beneath the shingles. I liked ripping away great swaths, shingle grains sliding off the roof, warm tar oozing at the edges. By the end of the day, blisters inflated my palms. My skin grew so slick with sweat, my clothes slid and drooped on my body.

In the evenings, my father climbed the ladder and inspected my work. He walked the ridge of the house, pointing out nails to hammer into place or little curls of shingle stuck in the gutters. He worked as a pole climber for the telephone company so he was excellent with heights. My balance was not so good as his. I scuttled after him on my haunches, crab-daughter with blackened hands. I could see mosquitoes quivering like TV static at the edges of his arms. They probed me as well, and I stopped still, letting them fasten on.

We didn't talk much inside the house. I made a dish with cabbage and onions, and my father spooned it on toast. The dog arranged her spine against the door, rolling her skull again and again on the knob. She missed my grandfather. I tried to explain he was gone, talking to the dog the way my mother used to: in complete sentences. Once years ago I caught my mother explaining to the dog the concept of weekends. She said, *On certain special days, honey, we sleep late. On those days you get to stay in your crate and dream a little longer.* I remember my grandfather walked in and rolled his eyes. *For Christ's sake, she either pees herself or doesn't.* My mother frowned. She said to the dog, *Well, doesn't that clear things up? Pee yourself, honey, go right ahead. I'm sorry to bother you, let me get out of your animal way.*

I know that talking to the dog can be a sneaky way to talk to someone else.

To Coco at the door, I said, "It's just us for now. We're good enough."

My father said, "Don't forget Orson." Orson was the cat.

One night the power went out, and Dad stuck some birthday candles in a loaf of bread. They were the only candles in the house, and we hovered over them expectantly. They made rippled skirts of wax on the crust of the bread. Dad rolled a battery from a broken flashlight on his palm. Outside the dark windows, I could feel the beautiful empty houses rise up, nudging the trees with their rooftops. Then the last candle snuffed out, and my father sat silent in the dark. I couldn't see him until he shifted in his chair, emerging from the general blackness.

When I met my mother for lunch, she wanted to know what my father said about her. I didn't want to say *nothing at all*, so I told her other things that were true: he didn't eat as well, he slept poorly. My mother, beaming, took these as compliments. We ate lunch at places she couldn't afford, restaurants near the new golf course where we chose salads from the appetizer list. The salads were composed of complicated, pretty foliage. We shivered in the air conditioning.

"He doesn't know who he is," she insisted. "He doesn't *know* he doesn't know."

My mother had gone to work since I'd seen her last. She'd started selling cosmetics at a department store, and she was experimenting with her face. The tape from her eye job was gone, but now the skin across her cheeks was puffy and orange with makeup.

"Listen," she said, setting a lacy leaf on her tongue. "He's got aspirations, doesn't he? He thinks, this is what I am, a son. Even when his dad leaves, he just goes on being a son, not a husband. Not a father. For some reason, he can't stop being what he's been all his life. He's acting like a child."

"Sure," I said. "He misses Grandpa."

"Of course he misses him!" My mother glared at me. "But it's not as if the old guy's on a fishing trip or something. Your dad keeps working at that house like he's going to surprise his daddy when he gets back."

I thought of all the windowpanes I'd scraped and painted. The new white door. "I think it's *nice*. He's fixing it *up*."

"For what? For a dead man?"

I squeezed my cloth napkin. "Grandpa's not dead."

"Not yet. If your father visited Ron more often, he'd know better than to fix up a house for him. *I* visited him."

"Grandpa?"

"That's what I'm saying." She sucked from her straw and looked at me. "I sat by his bed and watched him open and close his mouth. Like a fish."

The waiter came by with a tray of pie slices and dessert breads. He was charming and effusive, calling me *lady* but talking only to my mother. He wanted us to order more than salads.

When he left, my mother whispered hopefully, "Do you think he'd give me a ride someplace?"

"The waiter?"

"Your dad."

She was forever coming back to him, as if he were our one mutual friend and we had nothing else in common. I splayed my hands out on the white tablecloth. They were stained black with tar from the roof.

"You'll have to ask him about that."

"What's wrong with your hands?"

I spread my fingers farther out. They looked like something that lived in a swamp. I wanted to be chastised for bringing them to a fine restaurant.

But my mother was busy wiping a crumb from her lip with her pinkie finger. She was writing out the check. "Did you hear about that burned girl?" she asked. "Awful."

I pulled my hands back to my lap. Breezily: "She got fucked up."

The burned girl had been one of Julie's new friends, a year or two younger than the rest, but with a bigger chest than any of them. Before she was burned, I'd seen her linger after the pool closed, helping Julie carry her magazines and clothes. On the street, she was the one boys yelled at when they drove past in their cars. She could blush like no one I'd ever known, her skin a flash of red like something switched on, a buried bulb. After she was burned, her face was slippery and translucent and not really any color at all.

Her boyfriend said she put her head in a candle. He said, they were sitting in the dark, and she dipped her face down as if taking a drink, just a little sip and her hair was on fire.

The burned girl wasn't pitiable like Julie. She unnerved people with her bandaged face, made people uncertain of themselves, as if she'd accused them of something. Three weeks after she was burned, she walked hand in hand with her boyfriend in the park, tiny petals of translucent skin crinkling out from under her bandages. She made people feel guilty for having nice faces. Boys, the ones who used to jeer at her from their cars, followed her around furtively when she went shopping with her mother. They were busboys, they were baggers. If she caught them staring, they grew embarrassed and tried to open doors for her. They rummaged around in bins and found the best fruit: sleek apples, kiwis dripping with ice. They wanted her to touch them with her hand, to forgive them and bless them with her lipless glance. She took their fruit, but would say nothing. She only had one expression.

When the seniors asked Julie to sign a sympathy card for the burned girl, Julie refused. "It's insulting," she said (I heard this from my mother's friend at the pharmacy). "I'm sorry, but she did it to herself."

From my father's rooftop, I could see down the street and into the golf course pool. That's where Julie lay, surrounded by her most loyal girls. Their bright towels on the white patio chairs looked like the flags of nations. Annie was there, with her plum-red hair, and Kitty Roster, white and bonier than I remembered. Julie, in the center of them all, fanned herself with a fashion magazine. She made the healthier girls nervous and guilty, the ones splashing in the pool, so they climbed out of the water and didn't swim as many laps. They set straws between their teeth and sucked juices. They coughed when Julie coughed.

By that time, I'd nearly finished the roof. I spread tar paper over the smooth boards on the rafters, making a clean, black landscape up there—one I couldn't touch in the afternoon because it was so hot. It seemed like the surface of another planet, black and baking with underground fires. I liked how foreboding it was. My father planned to hire professionals to put the shingles down, a team of Mexicans from a company in town that did a roof a day. I told my father I could do it, but he looked at me like I'd made that joke before and it wasn't funny. He wrote me out a check instead. In the space for my name my father wrote Cash.

The day the Mexicans came, I climbed up in the neighbor's tree and watched them unload supplies. They had jeans and bare backs; they didn't speak Spanish; they all wore long, scraggly ponytails.

On the roof they did not scuttle or crawl. They strode across that black surface as if it were the land where they were born, familiar as their own backyards where they threw out garbage and buried animals. From time to time, they lit cigarettes and lifted their ponytails up, airing their necks.

By noon, they'd nearly covered my black planet. They sat on the front-yard grass and picnicked, sipping from water bottles and beer cans. They giggled at the dog, who came at them with her hackles up, dribbling urine. I climbed down from my tree.

"Well, look," they said. "Such a pretty squirrel."

"You shouldn't drink on the job."

"A pretty evangelist. Honey, you got bathroom?"

"Nope."

"No? We roofing a homestead or something? You take a piss with the dog in the grass?"

One of them opened a hand for the dog to sniff. He ran the other hand down the ridge of fur on her back, so slowly the bristles settled before he touched them. The dog leaned her jaw into his palm.

I took the dog by the collar and pulled her away. "My dad doesn't trust you."

"What, he's a racist or something?"

I paused, thinking of the way my father looked at me when I said I could do the roof myself. He hadn't even given me a chance. He'd said it would be too hard, too slow, to show me. I told them: "Actually, he's a narrow, small-minded man."

My father doesn't have any stories about Vietnam, so I made up one for him. It's not even a real war story. In it, he's just sitting on a bus in the middle of some city, staring out a dirty window at the bikes and meats and goats. I imagine him sliding around on one of those vinyl seats—the kind on school buses and café booths—and this Vietnamese woman is sitting next to him. She has nothing in her hands, no purse or bag or suitcase. She's pretty, but maybe she's been on the bus for a long time, because she's too tired to hold up her head. It rolls onto my father's shoulder. He starts to move away, so she murmurs something to him then in her language. I think he likes how her voice sounds. I think her head on his shoulder feels like a thousand pounds, and he wants to let her hold him down so he'll miss his stop, so he'll miss the war in the jungle and the flight back to America: the canary-yellow house that's waiting for him there, the storm windows he'll have to put in and take out, the hopeless teenage daughter and unhappy wife, the father he will never please enough.

He reaches out to touch the woman's hair, but she has only one word for him in English—*Yes*—so he freezes, pulls back. Waits. When she nods off again, he props her up against the window and changes seats. He gets off two stops early.

My father is a good man, but what do you do with all the good men in the world? There are too many already. Sometimes you want someone less good.

The burned girl came to high school orientation. I hadn't even realized she was in my class. I tried to think back to all the rooms and playgrounds we might have shared: the desks in rows, the tests so quiet you could hear the air conditioner. She sat in the bleachers with everyone else, though the people around her sat too close in order to seem like they weren't avoiding her. People had started to say she was creepy since she didn't act damaged. I could see the knuckly lobe of her ear, the patchy sheets of skin on her jaw like new bark. Her hair was growing back, bristly as a military cut, and as severe.

When her sweatshirt slipped between the bleachers, no one offered to get it for her. I half expected her to hobble, but she picked her way around backpacks and bodies, stepping carefully onto the basketball court. Her breasts bobbled under her T-shirt. I wondered where her boyfriend was, the one who walked with her while bits of her face drifted off in the park. Maybe he was older. Maybe he'd grown resentful of her like all the rest, like the boys she wouldn't blush for now, like Julie in her lounge chair counting vitamins on her thigh. People said Julie had invited the burned girl to her family's lake cottage, but the burned girl wouldn't come. Julie called her a snob: "It's not *nice* to snub people's pity," she said.

In the high school auditorium, the cheerleaders taught us the school song—Y-E-L-L-O-W-J-A-C-K-E-T-P-R-I-D-E—and then the Boy Scouts brought out the flag and wedged it between some folds in the theater curtains. The principal wanted to talk about the Pledge of Allegiance. He said, "It's important, in these controversial times, to remember why we make this oath to our country." I hadn't seen him since the summer funeral, and he looked tanned and well fed. "Wouldn't it be a shame," he said, "if because of those two words—'under God'—they called it a prayer and took this away from us too?"

The burned girl hadn't returned to the bleachers. People kept glancing down between their shoes, looking for her.

"You are citizens, and sons and daughters, and students at this school. How you coordinate these duties is your supreme responsibility." The principal scratched his nose. "It's going to be an exciting year."

A boy tossed a soda bottle through the basketball hoop. Its neck snagged in the ropes. The principal sipped from a milky glass of water. Beneath us all, the burned girl crawled in search of her sweatshirt. The room shook with sophomores standing up.

When the mascot climbed on stage, his bulging bee head under one arm like an astronaut's helmet, he put a hand on his belly instead of his heart. I put my hand on my belly, too.

When I got home from school, my mother was sitting at our kitchen table, four rolls of cotton in her mouth and her chin streaked with drool.

I said, "Mom?"

She said something plaintive, but all I understood was *holes* and *mouth*. My father, washing dishes at the sink, explained. She'd gotten four teeth extracted and was worried she'd be too woozy to take the bus. In a few weeks, she was getting corrective surgery on her jaw and braces.

My mother said, more clearly, "He was late."

My father turned off the sink and dried his hands on a paper towel.

"Ry dod en tong."

"What?" I didn't like looking at her. She pinched the bits of cotton from her mouth, slowly, like she was extracting the teeth all over again. Lines of drool thinned and broke, and she set the bloody wads on the table.

"Everybody went home, all the little girls with their mothers. They closed the place up. I had to sit outside the dentist's office on a curb and wait for him." She spat into a tissue.

My father said, "Watch out with that."

"I'm *bleeding*," my mother whined. I could see the sparkly blush on her cheeks, saved for occasions like these when people got very close to her face and examined her. She complained to my father, "I can't feel my *mouth!*"

My father didn't say anything else. He stayed close to the appliances, where there were small and continual tasks to perform with rags. He wiped crumbs and checked the bulb in the stove. When my mother said, "I feel like half my face is gone!" my father remembered a leak that needed fixing in the bathroom. My mother stared after him, crestfallen, as if he were abandoning her in the middle of their date.

She watched *Wheel of Fortune* with the dog, and I sat on the front steps and watched our new neighbors move in. They had a long white truck with a gaping door like the mouth of a deep tunnel.

Later, much later, my father came out of the bathroom and found my mother dozing on the couch. She had a small wad of tissues on her lap, arranged like a bouquet. My father stared at her for a second. Then my mother woke up and said, "Gabe!" blowing a bloody bubble of drool. My father looked horrified and sorry, which is something like love, maybe, so my mother was very pleased.

When she moved back in at the end of the summer, my mother didn't bring her miniatures in the tackle box. She brought cosmetics in plastic purses and cleaning equipment for her braces, tiny wire brushes and picks. My father was as wary of her as always, but he showed her the new spackle on the wall and the garbage disposal he installed for my grandfather. He flicked the switch and said, "Careful, careful. Okay?"

In the mornings, my mother likes grinding things up, the gurgle and crunch of half-eaten fruits, the quick disappearance of leftovers. She jumps and shrieks whenever she turns it on, as if it might take her hand down into the blades, as if she always wanted a sink with that sort of power. She says to my father, "Then you'd be stuck with me. Then you'd have to do the dishes while I watched!"

She holds up her perfect hand, and he steps back.

She laughs. "Sandra, Sandra, just look at him!"

I don't. I'm looking outside the window now, where the neighbors' lawns are going brown in stripes. Someone drags a sprinkler by a hose, wearily, never looking back. We've done this all before. My father is searching for a way out of the room, and I'm thinking, *Coward.* I'm thinking that riddle about the Indian at the courthouse is easy to solve. He just turned to the person with the hatchet next to him—someone he said he loved, who said he loved him—and held out both his arms.

But I don't think that's an impressive trick, not really. After the hands are gone, someone just puts shackles on your feet and you're back to where you started, only you can't eat soup or play cards. There's no escape in that. If it were me—! If it were me, I'd sit tight and let the bailiff lock the shackles around my wrists. I'd let him lead me into the courthouse and away from the soldiers who caught me in the fields, away from my buddies behind their painted shields, away from my family, who'd only pity me without hands, who'd have to bathe and feed me the rest of my helpless life. I'd let the bailiff lead me down the stairs into the dark cell under the courthouse, beneath the city, and that would be the trick: that I'd go willingly and never come back.

Outside, the neighbor is arranging a line of sprinklers in his grass. I open the door, and the dog leaps over the spray like fences, one after another after the next.

ACKNOWLEDGMENTS

These stories have appeared previously, sometimes in different forms, in the following publications: "Expecting" in *Boston Review*, "Catapult" in *The Chariton Review*, "One You Run from, the Other You Fight" in *Sou'wester*, "Marco Polo" in *New Delta Review* (and reposted on *Longreads* and *Instafiction*), "Gimme Shelter" (then titled "Raising the House") in *Great River Review*, "Lock Jaw" in *ZYZZYVA*, "Here, Still" in *New Orleans Review*, "Time Difference" in *FiveChapters*, and "Learning to Work with Your Hands" (then titled "Holiday") in *Philadelphia Stories*. I am grateful to the editors of these journals, who coaxed these stories into stronger versions.

I also extend my sincere thanks to Sarah Gorham, Ariel Lewiton, Kristen Radtke, and all those at Sarabande who believed in these stories and helped me bring them out into the world together as a collection. My very humblest thank you to Ben Marcus for reading *Catapult* and articulating with such grace what I had always only hoped a reader might find in its pages. I am also grateful to the supportive colleagues and devoted teachers who read these stories in their initial incarnations, in particular

Aimee Bender and T. C. Boyle when I was at the University of Southern California, and Marshall Klimasewiski and Kellie Wells when I was at Washington University in St. Louis. Thank you to both institutions for providing support, along with rich, enlivening writing communities in which to grow. Many thanks, too, to the Anderson Center and the Kimmel Harding Nelson Center for the Arts, where several of these stories were initially composed.

My gratitude to Nick Admussen for being such an intimate part of the long evolution of these stories: for your thrilling conversation, intense partnership, sharp intelligence, and ongoing friendship. So many of these works are so much better for your having read them.

And finally, this book owes its deepest debt to my family. This collection, at its core, comes out of a commitment I learned at an early age to care fiercely, while never forgetting to honor ambivalence, too, and its curious exploration of the many, many possible outcomes to every story. Thank you to my beloved parents and siblings for making art—chastening and so mysterious—possible in my life. It has been and *is* the most extraordinary gift.

SOME NOTES

Many books and ideas inspired this collection of stories, but there are some sources referred to or used more directly. "Catapult": information on time travel found on *Wikipedia*'s "Time Travel" entry, summer 2009. "Gimme Shelter": Lynn's boyfriend sings the Rolling Stones' song "Gimme Shelter." "Lock Jaw": The narrator's brother reads from the third step of *Twelve Steps and Twelve Traditions*. "Time Difference": Jill and her boyfriend discuss *The National Parks: America's Best Idea*, produced by Ken Burns and Dayton Duncan; Jill also reads from Richard Scarry's *Cars and Trucks and Things That Go*. "Old House": Liv quotes from *Heaven and Hell* by Emanuel Swedenborg.

ABOUT THE AUTHOR

Emily Fridlund grew up in Minnesota and currently lives in the Finger Lakes region of New York. Her fiction has appeared in a variety of journals, including *Boston Review, ZYZZYVA, FiveChapters, New Orleans Review, Sou'wester, New Delta Review, Painted Bride Quarterly,* and *Southwest Review.* She holds a PhD in Literature and Creative Writing from the University of Southern California. Fridlund's first novel, *History of Wolves* (Atlantic Monthly Press), was a Barnes & Noble Discover Great New Writers Selection, a *New York Times* Editor's Choice, one of *USA Today*'s Notable Books, an Amazon Best Book of the Month, and a #1 Indie Next pick.

SARABANDE BOOKS is a nonprofit literary press located in Louisville, KY, and Brooklyn, NY. Founded in 1994 to champion poetry, short fiction, and essay, we are committed to creating lasting editions that honor exceptional writing. For more information, please visit sarabandebooks.org.